SCOUT'S LEGACY

Charon MC
Book 7

KHLOE WREN

Books by Khloe Wren

Charon MC:
Inking Eagle
Fighting Mac
Chasing Taz
Claiming Tiny
Chasing Scout
Tripping Nitro
Scout's Legacy

Fire and Snow:
Guardian's Heart
Noble Guardian
Guardian's Shadow
Fierce Guardian
Necessary Alpha
Protective Instincts

Dragon Warriors:
Enchanting Eilagh
Binding Becky
Claiming Carina
Seducing Skye
Believing Binda

Jaguar Secrets:
Jaguar Secrets
FireStarter

Other Titles:
Fireworks
Tigers Are Forever
Bad Alpha Anthology
Scarred Perfection
Scandals: Zeck
Mirror Image Seduction
Deception
Mine To Bear

ISBN: 978-0-6483085-8-4
Copyright © Khloe Wren 2019

Cover Credits:
Models: Darrin Dedmon & John Wayne
Photographer: Jean Woodfin of JW Photography and Covers
Digital Artist: Khloe Wren
Editing Credits:
Editor: Carolyn Depew of Write Right

Acknowledgements

Writing Scout is always a pleasure, and I am so grateful that Scout and Marie's story lead to me being able to write a second book for them. This book is the first time I've ever written a second book for one of my couples, so was a new experience.

Massive thank you as always to my wonderful husband and girls who continue to put up with all the crazy things I do in order to get my books written in time.

I couldn't have written this book without several people who patiently answered all my many questions. Claudia, I'm sure at this point you regret that you let me know you're an EMT! Thank you for always answering my queries. Stacey and Brent, where would this book be without you both? I love the body disposal method we went with in the end.

By beta readers, Andrea, Miranda and Tracey, thank you for taking the time to help me get Scout's Legacy right.

I'm quite certain there were more people that helped me with this one and I'm sorry if I missed you by name here but know that I appreciate everyone who has helped me.

To my editor, Carolyn, no matter what I throw at you, you always come through with a marvelous edit. And this one was almost last minute, but not quite. One day I'm going to shock the pants off you and give you a book with plenty of time left on the clock! I appreciate everything you do and thank you for another job well done.

And of course, a huge thanks to my fb sprint group, the Night Writers, thank you all for the many, many sprints that got this baby done. To my street team, Khloe's Kickass Bikers, Beasties and Babes, thank you for all your love and support.

xo

Khloe Wren

Biography

Khloe Wren grew up in the Adelaide Hills before her parents moved the family to country South Australia when she was a teen. A few years later, Khloe moved to Melbourne which was where she got her first taste of big city living.

After a few years living in the big city, she missed the fresh air and space of country living so returned to rural South Australia. Khloe currently lives in the Murraylands with her incredibly patient husband, two strong willed young daughters, an energetic dog and two curious cats.

As a child Khloe often had temporary tattoos all over her arms. When she got her first job at 19, she was at the local tattooist in the blink of an eye to get her first real tattoo. Khloe now has four, two taking up much of her back.

While Khloe doesn't ride a bike herself, she loves riding pillion behind her husband on the rare occasion they get to go out without their daughters.

Dedication

To Stacey and Brent,
who needs google when I have you both?

Charon:

Char·on \ˈsher-ən, ˈker-ən, -än\

In Greek mythology, the Charon is the ferryman who takes the dead across either the river Styx or Acheron, depending on whether the soul's destination is the Elysian Fields or Hades.

Chapter 1

Scout

Even if I lived for a hundred years, I'd never get tired of waking up like this. With my son kicking at the palm I had resting over my old lady's rounded belly. Our boy was strong, that's for sure. I moved my hand, stroking over Marie's soft skin gently until he settled down his morning football practice.

Despite having woken up with a hard-on that was throbbing for some relief, I didn't want to wake her. Growing our baby boy was really wearing my girl out and he did a good job of keeping her awake during the night. I wasn't a heavy sleeper so knew there were often nights she tossed and turned for hours, unable to get comfortable. Glancing over her to the clock that sat on the table beside the bed, I saw it was still early. We had maybe another two hours, if we were lucky, before Ariel would be up and around.

Just thinking about my adopted daughter brought a smile to my lips. That little girl may not have an ounce of my DNA in her, but she was mine and if anyone ever dared hurt her, I'd rain hell down on them like they'd ever dream possible. She'd already been through so much in her young life. Her first lessons were to be unseen and unheard. When we first took her in seven months ago, she barely spoke. Born into a compound where she was the only child, we had no idea which of the fuckers out there was her biological father. Her mother, Sarah, had been the only woman and they'd been testing a drug on her, a drug that not only made her horny and lowered her inhibitions, but it also fucked with her memory. Poor Sarah. Guilt swamped me. She was Marie's foster sister and twenty-six years ago, when they'd gotten into trouble at a party at the Iron Hammers MC clubhouse, their foster father had brought them to me to keep safe. Fine fucking job I did of it.

After their ordeal with the Hammers, Sarah had been scared of all bikers. She'd left within a month of arriving and hadn't looked back. Marie had been gutted, but had refused to leave with her foster sister. Then, last year all hell broke loose and she turned up. The leader of the cult she'd fallen in with came after me. Stupid fucker took me off the side of the road when he caught me riding alone. Turned out the Iron Hammers had taken his sister and destroyed her, and the stupid bastard blamed the girls for the fact they got free while his sister didn't. It was a complete clusterfuck. I was used as bait to get Marie and Sarah and Marie fell for the trap. My boys came after us, but got there too late to save Sarah. She'd been injured and died in the hospital a few days later. After all she'd been through, it was probably a blessing, but it had left little Ariel an orphan.

Before Sarah died, she'd woken from her coma briefly and told Ariel that she should stay with me and Marie, that we would take care of her and she could trust us. We hadn't realized Ariel could even talk before she'd whispered a few words to her mother. And even after Sarah told her she could trust us, she didn't speak to us. She was more like a mouse than a child, sneaking around everywhere, trying not to be seen or heard. The poor girl was only a child. Originally, we'd all thought she was around two, but once we found Sarah's diary, we discovered she was actually four. Years of not eating properly, not getting enough sunlight or fresh air, had taken its toll, stunting her growth. She'd turned five last month, and thankfully she's grown some since we took her in. I'd never thought I'd be so excited to buy little girl clothing, but twice she's needed a bigger size, and Marie and I were overjoyed. Our daughter was getting better, and we were hoping like hell she wouldn't have issues in adulthood from her rough start.

I'd never forget those early days and weeks when she would eat everything she could get her hands on before dashing off to hide in her room. None of us had any idea what she'd really been forced to suffer through in that fucking compound, but watching her recover from it made me want to kill each one of those fuckers all over again for what they'd done to her.

With a small moan, Marie wriggled her ass against me, rubbing over my already hard cock, making it twitch. Unsure if she was awake or asleep, I held still, trying to decide what to do next. I'd love nothing more than to roll her over and slide in deep, but she needed her rest more than I needed to fill her up. Maybe. To be honest, in my mind, it was a close call on which was the more pressing need.

Her hand slipped over my hip until she could dig her fingers into my ass and pull me in tight against her. Realizing she was, in fact, awake, my blood heated and I grinned as I nuzzled my face in against her throat while shifting my palm up to cup her breast. I gently rubbed my thumb over her nipple—pregnancy had not only made her tits bigger—it made them super sensitive, so I made sure I was always careful not to hurt her with my playing.

I kissed my way up her neck until my mouth was over her ear.

"Morning, love."

"Hmmm."

She squirmed against me, trying to push me, but I didn't budge. I knew she wanted me to shift over to allow her to roll over onto her back, but I had other ideas. Running a hand down her body, I lifted her leg and hooked it back over mine. With another of her little moans, she got what I wanted and tilted her ass back at me. Trailing my fingers down her inner thighs, I then ran them over her pussy, growling at the moisture I found.

"You're so fucking wet, babe. What were you dreaming of?"

"I was down at the beach staring over the water, when…" she paused for a moment as I slipped two fingers inside her and began to tease her. "Jason Ma—Hey!"

Her words cut short when, with a growl, I pulled my fingers out of her heat and gave her inner thigh a sharp tap.

"Woman, that's not nice."

She was giggling as she reached a hand back to run through my hair and pull my face in against her neck. "Sugar, you know full well you're the only one who gets me worked up like this. And you do it by just being yourself. I wasn't dreaming of anything, simply waking up in your arms does this to me."

"That's a much better answer."

I didn't let her get another word in before I shifted, then thrust forward and buried my cock deep within her soft, slick core. Our moans filled the air when I pulled back and thrust back in again.

"I'll never get enough of you, of this. I love you, Marie. So fucking much."

She arched her body, tilting her hips back and taking me deeper.

"Back at you, Charlie. Love you more each day."

I can't believe I was so stupid I nearly missed out on this. I have no clue what the fuck I was thinking, ignoring what we had for over two decades, but now I'd woken the fuck up, I was all for making the most of every moment. Needing to see her face, I pulled free of her body and rolled her over onto her back. Cupping her face in my palm, I took her mouth with mine, kissing her deeply, until she was moaning and squirming beneath me. When her hand snaked down and gripped me, my cock twitched against her palm as a groan tore from my throat. I pressed my lips to hers once more before I pulled back and shifted until I was kneeling between her thighs. I let my gaze run over her body. From her messed-up hair and half closed eyes, to her belly swollen with my son growing inside her, down to her slick pussy that was wet and waiting for me, she was the sexiest thing I'd ever seen. And she was all mine.

Taking my cock in my fist, I stroked myself twice as I smirked at her, stroking my beard with my other hand as she grew restless. I loved teasing my woman. She was a sight to see all riled up.

"Stop teasing me already!"

A ripple ran over her belly and my attention zeroed in on it instantly, my focus shifting from my cock to my son. My heart softened as I rested both my palms over her stomach, stroking our son as he rolled around within her. The breath froze in my lungs for a few moments. Even after all these months I could scarcely believe we'd created a life, that Marie was so fucking perfect that she could take my seed and grow a baby within her with it.

Tears pricked my eyes as I leaned in and pressed a kiss to my woman's belly. I'd never be able to thank her for everything she'd gifted me, for the way she'd forgiven me for all the shit I pulled and took me in. Made me fucking whole and giving me a family I hadn't realized I'd needed.

Marie
In an instant, all levity evaporated from between us. Our boy had rolled over, his knee or maybe his elbow, raising my skin as it shifted around, gaining Scout's full attention instantly. The laughter vanished from his gaze as he caressed my stomach, soothing our son with his big hands. As serious as the moment was, it didn't cool down my arousal for my husband. Nope—if anything, it increased it. Seeing this big, strong man completely humbled by the fact his baby was growing inside my womb did things to me.

"Charlie…"

My voice broke with emotion. This man was the center of my universe, had been for decades, but now that he was officially mine, it was different. Better. No more of only being able to dream of how it would feel. Now I could wake up and with a roll of my hips, have him inside me. Life with Scout and Ariel was so much better than what I'd had before. All I'd had was my cafe and empty dreams. My pining for this man had nearly driven me over the edge, but it had been worth it. Every single thing we'd been through had been worth it, because it had led to this. We were living together, married, with a daughter and were pregnant with a son.

He lifted up from kissing my stomach to gaze up to my face. His eyes shone with unshed tears and my heart melted.

"Make love to me, Charlie. I need you."

I needed the connection I only felt when he was inside me. Nothing beat how it felt to have his thick length stroking within me while his big body hovered over me.

Without taking his gaze from mine, he moved with smooth efficiency, sliding his hard erection into me. I felt every ridge as he slowly glided in, taking his time, clearly enjoying me squirming beneath him. I tilted my hips, trying to get him to go deeper, faster. He was driving me nuts with his teasing today.

"Shh, Marie. Let me love you right."

He leaned forward, holding his weight on one arm as he cupped my face with the other. My belly pressed against his as he leaned down and gently kissed me, his lips teasing mine. It wasn't enough. When he tried to move away, I threaded my fingers in his hair and pulled him back for more. He kept the slow pace of thrusting his dick deep within me as he ate at my mouth. He nipped and licked between kisses until I was drunk on him and my hands loosened their grip, allowing him to pull back to kneel between my thighs. He ran a palm over my stomach, grinning when our boy nudged his hand.

"Love you, Marie. So fucking perfect."

Tears pricked my eyes as I stared up at my man, his muscles bunching and releasing as he kept his movements slow and steady. He was so damn beautiful, and this slow lovemaking had my arousal gently building as it curled through me. It was sweet and gentle, but I wanted more, needed more this morning.

"I love you too, Charlie. But you're driving me crazy with this slow and steady thing. Please, babe, I need you to take me. Own me."

He smirked, tilting his head down until he could look at me through his eyelashes.

"But if we keep it slow, I can keep at you all fucking day, and I don't ever want to stop."

I chuckled at that and glanced over at the clock.

"I think Ariel's a little young for the sex talk, so you'll have to save tormenting me all day long for another time."

His body tensed for a moment, as though he'd forgotten we had a little person in the house who liked to come and say good morning when she got up.

"Fuck."

His rough hands gripped my hips and his movements sped up. I nearly sighed in relief as he leaned forward and got serious about taking me. I ran my hands over his face, gave his beard a tug, then ran my palms down his arms where I gripped his biceps as he took me just like I wanted him to. The faster movement had me spiraling toward my climax, but before I could go over, he growled and pulled out of me. Before I could ask what the hell he was doing, he had me flipped over and on all fours, running a palm over my stomach, making sure it wasn't pressed against the mattress, before he moved in behind me.

"Hold on, babe, and no screaming. I don't want Ariel scared."

A blush heated my face. Soon after Ariel had moved in he'd made me scream loud enough that the next morning Ariel had refused to be anywhere near him, or speak. Worried about what had happened I had a talk with her, and eventually got her to tell me she'd been scared he'd hurt me and she didn't know how to deal with him after that. Poor little love.

With a hand wrapped around the back of my neck possessively, he thrust in deep, drawing a moan from me as heat flared through my body. He set a fast and furious pace, my mind emptying of all thoughts aside from the pleasure rapidly building within me. Turning my head, I buried my face against my arm, muffling the sounds I couldn't help but make as my man showed me exactly who was the master of my body.

With a low growl, he shifted a hand under me, finding my clit and teasing the little nub until my body stiffened and I flew apart, crying out against my arm as he thrust in a few more times before holding himself deep. His dick twitched within me as he came.

Once he was spent, he pulled free and gently guided me over so I was laying on my side. Lost in bliss, I let my eyes close and was only vaguely aware of him cleaning me up and spooning up behind me.

It was later that I woke again, a small hand slipping into mine. As sweet a gesture as her wanting to hold my hand was, it still scared the shit out of me every time. There was something spooky about being woken up like that, but I couldn't tell her not to do it. I refused to risk setting her back with such a comment.

"Hey, sweet angel, you sleep well?"

She nodded and glanced down at my belly, as she did every morning since I'd started showing. I threw back the blankets, leaving just the sheet covering me. Ariel shifted so she could rest her little head against me, her ear pressed up against the sheet. She'd told us she could hear her little brother, that he told her secrets. The first time she'd mentioned it, Scout freaked the fuck out, but I thought it was sweet—and imaginary. I was quite sure my boy wasn't talking to his sister just yet. Ariel was completely enthralled with her baby brother already and I knew she'd be an awesome, mostly likely, over-protective big sister to him. Just like she already was with the other Charon babies. I couldn't wait to watch them together as they grew older.

Scout buried his face in my neck, his beard tickling my skin as he kissed me. Then he reached over to run a palm over Ariel's hair. The contrast between his darkly tanned skin and her white-blonde hair had me mesmerized for a few moments.

"Morning, angel. You ready for breakfast?"

After pressing a kiss to my tummy and whispering something too quietly for me to hear, she turned a big grin up to Scout.

"Oh, yes. Waffles!"

Not waiting for an answer, she flew off the bed and out of the room, leaving me chuckling, along with Scout.

"Can't believe how far that kid's come so fast. You want some waffles too, babe?"

I rolled over and ran a palm over his cheek, before stroking my fingers through his beard, twirling some hair around one and giving it a small tug.

"She is a marvel. And I'd love some. I need to head into the cafe this morning. Do you think you could watch Ariel for a few hours?"

I had pies to take in, and it would be much faster if I could do it on my own. After turning to press a kiss to my palm, he smiled as he moved to get out of bed, which gave me a great look at his very fine ass before he dressed and covered the view.

"Sure, babe. We'll just hang out here and have some daddy-daughter time. I'll go get a start on the waffles so you can get cleaned up in peace."

The twinkle in his eyes told me he'd much rather help me in the shower than go cook, but that wasn't going to happen this morning. Not now a certain little girl, who had Scout firmly wrapped around her finger, had made her breakfast demands known. He couldn't resist her. None of us could. I ran a palm over my belly. Soon there would be two in the house making demands on us.

I couldn't wait.

Chapter 2

Scout

I couldn't help but smile as I watched Ariel pour syrup over her waffle. The serious expression on her little face as she squeezed the bottle got me every time. Then, when the liquid dropped onto her breakfast, filling the holes in the waffle before leaking over the edges, she grinned and a small chuckle escaped. I fucking loved how she enjoyed the little things. Ariel was such a serious child most of the time, getting her to laugh—hell, even smile—had become my daily challenge. And I vowed I'd never stop doing it, never stop finding ways to make this little girl light up.

It had taken weeks before she'd relaxed around food. To start with, she'd sneak out during the night and raid the kitchen, stashing all sorts of things in her room. After the stench of rotten food revealed what she'd been doing, we sat her down and explained that she didn't need to hoard food like that. That she could go to the kitchen to get whatever she wanted when she was hungry. Marie also pointed out that if she ate food that she'd hidden in her room and left to go bad, she'd get very sick.

Thankfully we got the message through to her and we hadn't smelled any new surprises since. I loved that now she was enjoying food, not just eating all she could whenever she could, it opened up all sorts of edible adventures we could take together. I was about to ask her if she wanted to make a cake while Marie was out when my phone rang. Glancing at the screen I saw it was Mac so, with a wince as I wondered what the fuck had gone wrong now, I answered it right away.

"Mornin', Mac. What's up?"

"Nothing good. Just got word from a friend back home that you're gonna want to know about asap."

By back home, Mac meant Los Angeles. Which, given his past, meant it was mob related. Just fucking great. John Bennett, the father of my VP's niece, and Eagle's old lady, Silk, had fucked with the L.A. mob before he'd died and they'd come after her over it a while back, but we'd sorted that shit and she was now settled in with Eagle and their son. That shit had gone down two years ago and we hadn't heard dick from them since we'd dealt with the fuckers. I had no clue what would have caused them to come after us now.

"How urgent? I've got Ariel with me."

"It's about as urgent as it gets, but it's definitely not child-friendly information."

A warm palm on my arm had me turning to face Marie.

"I'll take her with me. I think Zara's going to have Cleo with her, and Ariel loves to play with her. Isn't that right, Ariel? You want to come into the cafe with me for a little while? Then maybe afterward we can come back here and you can help me bake something?"

Our daughter's face lit up as she nodded and I knew it was a go.

"Okay, Mac. That's all sorted. I'm on my way to the clubhouse now. Do we need everyone there?"

"Your call, prez. I'm not sure how fast the other side is gonna act."

Non-secure phone lines were a bitch.

"Okay, I'll just call in Bulldog, Keys, Arrow and Nitro for now. We can easily call in the others if we need to."

"Good deal. See you soon, prez."

Hanging up the phone, I pulled up a text and tapped a message to my VP, Secretary, Treasurer and SAA telling them to get their asses to church asap. Then I pocketed my phone and pulled Marie around in front of me.

"Sorry, babe. Be careful today, not sure what Mac's heard, but just be extra careful, yeah?"

"Always, Scout. But you do the same."

Cupping her face, I leaned down to kiss her deeply, letting her taste fill my senses for a moment. With a sigh, I pulled back from her but before she could step away from me, I dropped down to give her tummy a kiss.

"You be good for your mom, young man."

That got a chuckle from both my ladies. I scooped Ariel up off her seat to give her a tickle-hug before putting her back and pressing a kiss to her temple.

"And I'll see you later, angel. I'll see what I can do about having some lunch at the cafe with you both, sound good?"

She gave a nod and leaned up to press a light kiss to my cheek. She didn't like the feel of my beard against her lips, so the few times she wanted to show me some love, it was always high on my cheek or on my forehead. She was doing it more often now, and I loved and cherished every one of her kisses.

With my mind already churning over what the fuck could be coming our way now, I left my girls happily eating breakfast and made my way out to my bike. I had a bad feeling about what Mac was bringing to the table. Fuck, I hoped whatever it was would be done with before my son was born. I wanted to be able to take a little time off from the club and enjoy it at home with Marie, Ariel and our boy. Not chasing after some fuckers who thought they could take on the Charon MC and win. After scrubbing a hand over my face, I snatched up my helmet and headed out.

Twenty minutes later I was sitting in church with my closest friends and brothers around me while Mac paced the floor in front of us.

"Mac, brother, just spit it out already."

With a huff, Mac came over and placed his hands on the table, leaning forward until he was staring me in the eye.

"The last book is coming into play."

Fuck. I was right, this was gonna be big and messy.

"The Ice Riders?"

"Yeah."

For a long time before John Bennett died, he'd been gathering secrets and financial information on several organizations, and writing it all down in ledgers. None of us had any fucking clue until two years back, when it was discovered that his bag had missed the flight that ended his life. Somehow the L.A. mob had worked out what he'd been up to, so when they'd heard about the bag they'd come after Silk, kidnapping her so they could get their hands on the thing. Naturally, things didn't go as planned for them—or us, and we ended up with six fucking ledgers full of dirty deeds. John had collected shit on the L.A. mob, the Satan's Cowboys MC, the Iron Hammers MC, the N.Y. mob, the Ice Riders MC and us. In order to get the L.A. mob off our backs, we'd handed over copies of their ledger and the N.Y. ledger. The Iron Hammers had changed leadership over a year ago and were now friendly with us, so that ledger was dead in the water. The Satan's Cowboys MC was a large club that pretty much controlled Texas. If you wanted to be an MC in this state, you had to play nice with them. We'd handed over their ledger in order to strike a deal that kept them from dealing drugs in Bridgewater. The only book left untouched was the Ice Riders MC, who were a club up in Boston that we knew fuck all about, as we'd never had anything to do with them. To be honest, I had no fucking clue how word would have gotten to them that the ledger we had on them even existed, let alone that we were in possession of it.

Nitro voiced my thoughts. "How'd they even find out about it? I don't think any of our boys have ever even met anyone from their club before."

Mac turned to face Nitro. "Guess there was something in the L.A. mob's ledger that referred to it, or maybe in the New York book we gave them. No fucking idea, but we knew Sabella wasn't gonna stay gone forever with how we left shit. He's always going to be in the background, looking for ways to fuck us over."

Yeah, the mob boss hadn't been happy that we'd handed him his ass with what went down with Silk. Don't think he'd ever gone up against an MC before and he wasn't prepared for us to fight back like we had.

"You saying Sabella went to this club? Told them we got dirt on them?"

"I got a call this morning letting me know that not only did Sabella tell them we had John's book on them, but that we were gearing up to do something about it."

I groaned and ran a hand through my hair. Fuck me.

"So naturally they're gonna turn up on our fucking doorstep to strike first, right?"

"Somethin' like that."

I turned to Keys. "Call everyone in for church this afternoon. We need this shit out in the open so everyone's on the lookout. Nitro, sort out the prospects to cover the women when they're moving around. Once we deal with these jokers, we need to figure out a way to handle Sabella permanently. He's declared war on us with this shit, and I ain't lettin' it stand."

Marie

After giving Ariel one of the pies to carry inside, I grabbed the bag with the rest of them, then followed her into my cafe. Ariel was so sweet with how she loved to help out. She took every job given to her with the seriousness of brain surgery. In a way, it saddened me how solemn she was most of the time, but it was also completely adorable to see her in her mission mode, getting shit done. She was going to be a force to be reckoned with by the time she was a teen. *Lord help us.*

As my pregnancy progressed, I'd handed over more and more of the day-to-day stuff to Zara. These last few weeks had really hit me hard. Being pregnant in your forties was not easy. My blood pressure wasn't the best and I got so damn tired so easily it was ridiculous. Thankfully both Zara and Mercedes were good, solid workers and I could trust them to take care of things. Zara was standing behind the counter setting things up for the day when we walked in. As soon as she saw us, she moved around to our side and lowered down to

Ariel's level when the little girl got to her with her pie held out proudly.

"And what flavor do we have today?"

"Blueberry. Mommy has cherry and apple ones, too."

"Wow, you went all out this week, huh?"

Ariel gave a serious bob of her head as Zara took the pie from her hands.

"You know, Cleo's over in the play-pen if you want to go say hi. It would be a big help if you could keep her busy for us. Do you think you could do that for me? Play with Cleo while Mommy and I get to work."

That got another nod before she turned and, with a grin on her little face, dashed over to the play-pen in the corner where Cleo sat banging two toys together.

"Not sure encouraging those two to form a bond is in our best interest, Zara. Can you imagine the trouble they'll get into later on?"

Zara laughed and took the bag from me, removing the other two pies and placing them into the display cabinet before I could even think of doing it myself.

"I'm pregnant, girl. Not an invalid. I'm more than capable of putting the damn things in the display."

Zara winced as she closed the door and folded the bag up.

"Scout got to you didn't he?"

"It's only for these last few weeks. He's worried you're trying to do too much. It's sweet, if you think about it."

Knowing there wasn't a damn thing I could do to change how Zara was going to spend the next few weeks, I just shook my head at her and made my way over to the coffee machine.

"Oh, um…"

Mercedes came out from the back room and made a move to stop me but I cut her down with a glare before she could finish her sentence.

"So help me, if you try to stop me from having my coffee… One cup. I get one damn cup of coffee each day. Do *not* come between me and it."

With wide eyes, she put her palms up and backed away and guilt rode me. Mercedes had first arrived in Bridgewater after she fled the cult she'd been raised in. She didn't handle making mistakes well, and always shut down hard if someone got mad at her. Since settling down with Tiny she'd gotten better, but she still had a long way to go. I reached out and rested a palm on her arm.

"Mercedes, I'm not mad at you, sugar. It's just been a long eight months growing this boy of mine, and I'm about done with Scout's over-protectiveness."

"How about you go sit down and I'll make it for you? I promise I won't use the decaf like Scout told me to."

That had me chuckling and I pulled her in for a hug, happy she was back to her normal self.

"Sure thing, sugar. It'll be our secret."

I moved out from behind the machine and took a seat at an empty table facing the kids, but not so close that they'd think I was hovering. Ariel didn't do well when she thought she was being watched. Poor love tried to do everything she thought adults would want her to do, not realizing we just wanted her to be a child and have fun with learning how to live her life free.

Apparently Scout had the whole damn universe out to prevent me getting my caffeine this morning, because before Mercedes could place the cup on the table in front of me, the front door crashed open. Naturally, the noise made her jump and the cup slipped, dropping to the floor and shattering. In reflex, I jumped up from my seat to avoid the hot liquid and quickly found myself with a thick arm around my throat. A chill ran down my spine and a wave of dizziness hit me when the barrel of a gun pressed against the side of my belly.

"Don't move."

Mercedes back-peddled, clearly in shock. A second man came in and pointed his weapon at her head. Seconds dragged on, feeling like a lot longer as panic shot through me. Forced into inaction, I stood useless with a gun pressed against my unborn son and an arm so tight around my throat I struggled to get enough air in my lungs as I watched what went down. Without moving my head, I glanced to the kids. They were okay. Relief flooded me that my beautiful, smart girl had already opened the play-pen and was carry-dragging Cleo, who had only just starting to walk, toward the counter. She looked up at me with wide, fear-filled eyes and I gave her a smile, hoping she took it as encouragement to keep going.

"You. Stop right there."

Zara was stumbling toward a table. Extreme emotion would bring on a cataplexy attack, and clearly she'd been trying to fight it off but couldn't any longer.

"Don't shoot her! She can't help it. She has medical conditions. Please, let Mercedes go to her before she collapses and hurts herself."

I risked a quick glance back to the girls, and Ariel's lips had firmed into a straight line as she glared at the man holding me. Then she made the most of Zara holding everyone's attention and silently disappeared behind the protection of the counter with little Cleo. Hopefully she was heading into the back room and through the newly added door into the neighboring shop that Cindy, Nitro's woman, ran. I had complete confidence Cindy would take care of the girls and call the club in to deal with these bastards.

When Zara crashed to the floor, I jerked against the man holding me and cried out for her. With no one to guide her fall, she hit hard, taking a chair down with her. Blood flowed from a cut on her face. I tried to pull forward to get to her, but his grip tightened as he growled low, near my ear. If only he didn't have his gun up against my stomach like he did, I'd have some hope of trying to break free of his grip. But I couldn't risk my son like that.

"Oh, for fuck's sake."

While the man holding his gun on Mercedes continued to curse up a storm, he didn't shift his aim. I guessed the one holding me was just here for muscle. He had barely moved, or made a sound since he'd grabbed me and told me not to move. The only blessing in all of this shit was that they'd allowed the few customers we'd had to flee when they'd first come in with their weapons out. It was just us three now that the kids had slipped away.

"Please, let Mercedes help her. Just—"

"Shut the fuck up and give me your fucking phone."

"It's in my bag. I can't reach it unless you get this one to let me go."

Without taking his gun off Mercedes, he came over and grabbed my bag off the floor near my feet and upended it on the table. Grabbing my phone from the mess he'd made, he handed it to me.

"Unlock it and pull up your man's number, but don't dial it. You dial, I'll start shooting."

The bastard holding me didn't loosen his hold on my neck so I held the phone up to unlock the screen, tap in my password, then pull up Scout's phone number. As I did that, the other guy had Mercedes sit next to Zara. But not to help her. Fucker pulled out zip ties and used them to tie Mercedes' hands together, around a leg of the table Zara was near.

He then came over and snatched my phone from my hand. "Put her over with the others."

As the one holding me shoved me forward, a shot of pain ripped through my lower belly and I cried out as I wrapped one arm around my stomach, and gripped a chair with the other one. Holy fuck, that hurt.

"Stop fucking around and get her tied up already, Tank."

"You see how far fucking pregnant she is, Rumble? Last thing this situation needs is her to go into fucking labor on us. Make the call. I'll deal with it."

Every word he said faded away except for one. Labor. I knew stress could bring on early labor. Since I was older, I was considered high risk so the doctor had explained all sorts of shit that could go wrong. Unfortunately while Scout was there, which was why he had the entire damn town treating me with kid gloves. I breathed through the pain and before I got a gun shoved against me again, I spoke as I moved.

"Could you let me sit in a chair rather than the floor?"

He sighed like he didn't want to, but could see that getting me on the floor wasn't going to be easy for either of us.

"Fine, just hurry up, 'k?"

Breathing through another jolt of pain that had me getting really worried, I lowered myself into the chair beside Mercedes. I ran my palm over her head when she leaned it against my thigh before I put my hands out for him to do whatever he was going to do with them. He was being somewhat gentle with me now and I didn't want to do anything that would make him get rough, especially if I really was about to go into early labor.

Putting the gun away, he set about using zip ties to secure my wrists to either side of the chair. I would have preferred have my hands to hold my aching stomach, but at least he didn't put them together behind my back. Another stab of pain rolled through me and with a groan I closed my eyes and prayed.

Chapter 3

Scout

Walking out of church, we all grabbed our phones and powered them on. Each one of them lit up like a fucking Christmas tree as they came online. Naturally, Keys was the first to get into his messages.

"Fuck, prez. We got trouble already."

My vision tunneled in on my phone as I read the text that flashed up. Cindy, Nitro's old lady, had sent a text out to each of us since she couldn't get anyone to answer a phone. Ariel had brought Cleo over through the back door, and she'd been distraught over "men with guns in the cafe with mommy." Looked like the Ice Riders were in town already.

"Nitro, call your girl. Bulldog, get on Tiny and get him to meet us there. Keys, get me the camera inside the cafe. Mac, you armed?"

His old lady, Zara was working in the cafe, as was Tiny's woman, Mercedes. This would be a good test of Mac's ability to stay calm under pressure. We hadn't made it public knowledge, but Bulldog was looking to step down soon from his role of VP, so we'd discussed who would take over and Mac was the front runner.

"Always, prez." He pulled out his knife and gun to show me before he tucked them both away, after double-checking his weapon was loaded and ready to go. Mac had been a Gunnery Sergeant in the Marines, so of course the man was armed and ready to roll. Gotta love a Marine.

I turned to Nitro, who'd just hung up from his call.

"She went out front and peeked in through the window. Two men armed with pistols have our women in there. No customers."

"Right, no time to waste. Keys, we'll need that feed up and live by the time we roll in." I looked around the room at the few brothers who had been hanging around before this shit hit the fan. They were all watching and waiting for my orders. It was good to be king. "Bash, need you to grab the bus and go get Donna on your way to the cafe. No matter how this pans out, I want Marie to go in to be checked over. Everyone else, on your bikes. We're rolling out as soon as I can start my fucking bike."

Donna was Keys' old lady and a nurse. The woman was a gem, always coming through for us.

Confident my orders would be followed, I headed out the door. Not wasting time with my helmet, I swung my leg over my ride and started it up. The moment I could, I peeled out of the lot and roared over to Marie's Cafe, praying I made it in time to save my heart.

With me disregarding my personal safety, I arrived a few minutes ahead of the rest of the club. My phone started vibrating as I killed the engine. Pulling it free, I saw Marie's number and a cold chill ran up my spine. I doubted this was actually my woman calling me. To answer or not? They were about to hear a whole heap of bikes roll in and realize we were onto them, so in order to keep an element of surprise in our favor, I declined the call and made my way around to the front of the building, Ideally, I would have liked to have seen where they were standing on the video feed, but the few minutes it was gonna take Keys to get here and get it loaded up could be minutes too long.

The sounds of a couple bikes pulling up behind the building, along with the sounds of the other bikes approaching, had me confident that I'd have back-up within moments, so I didn't stop or turn around as I marched up the pavement in front of the shop. A growl rolled up my throat when, through the glass, I saw some motherfucker strapping Marie's arms to a chair. My heart skipped a beat at the pinched expression on her face. She was in pain. Zara was out cold on the floor, blood on her face, while Mercedes was tied to the table near Marie. Girl had her head resting on Marie's thigh and the blank look on her face made me think this shit had triggered memories from her past that were messing with her head.

The second man had Marie's phone and was cursing up a storm as he hit buttons. Guess he didn't like me not answering.

Hearing boots running behind me, I knew I had armed back-up so didn't hesitate to shove the door open hard and fast and step inside.

"What the fuck do you two bastards think you're doing? Fucking with the Charon MC isn't good for your health, and taking three of our women—one heavily pregnant, really isn't good for your fucking health. You got less than thirty seconds to explain yourselves before my brothers start shooting."

My vision clouded red when the bastard who was tying up Marie pulled his gun and pressed it against her stomach. That shit-stain was a dead man for that move alone. Threatening an unborn baby. Fucker.

The asshole with the phone didn't bother pulling any weapon, like he didn't think we were a fucking threat. He just kept hold of Marie's phone as he ran his gaze over each of us. The one holding my woman spoke, drawing my attention back to him.

"I don't think you'll shoot us. Not when it'll put your kid at risk."

Rage continued to pulse through me, stealing my voice for a moment. Mac stepped up next to me, gun trained on the one with the phone.

"You went to a lot of trouble to get us here, boys. How about you quit wasting our time and tell us what you want?"

Mac was already acting like a VP, staying calm under pressure and having my back. I could see things working out well on that front. But in this moment all I could deal with was the gun pointed at my boy and the pain and panic on my old lady's face. I was so focused, I nearly missed when someone moved behind them. Oh, Nitro needed to get a handle on his fucking woman. Forcing my gaze from the scene, I turned to face the asshole with the phone, who was standing further forward in the room than his buddy, and since he was looking at Mac, he hadn't seen our little Harley Quinn wannabe coming in the back with a fucking baseball bat raised.

"Been told you were planning to use some fucking book John Bennett wrote on our business to blackmail us. We're here to make sure you understand that ain't happening."

"You don't know shit. We've had that fucking book for two years and haven't fucking touched it. You want it? You should have had your fucking president contact me and we could have sorted something out. This is not how you get favors, boy."

That had him pausing. What the fuck was going on here? Their cuts declared them Ice Riders MC, but I wanted to know who exactly sent these fuckers.

"Who sent you?"

"Our president, Chains. Told us to get down here and get shit sorted."

"And your first choice was to hold our women hostage? Not real fucking bright, are you?" I gave Cindy a nod and before these two assholes knew what was happening, one took a bat to the side of the head and Mac put a bullet in the other one a split second later. "Mac, don't fucking kill him. Need to ask some more questions and I think our resident Harley fucking Quinn, here, may have made it impossible to ask that one anything."

"I'd say I'm sorry, but it got the job done. Now, I'll leave you boys to it. I got two little ladies to go look after."

With that, she dashed up to Nitro to give him a quick kiss before she fled through the back room to return to her store.

"That's some woman you have, Nitro."

"One that's not gonna be able to sit comfortably for a while. Fuck me. When I saw her come in with that bat…"

I tuned them out and rushed to Marie, pulling out my knife as I went.

"Babe, where does it hurt? What'd he do to you?"

I cut her wrists free and she grabbed her belly and leaned forward, her head finding my shoulder.

"I think I'm in labor."

Icy fingers gripped my heart and I squeezed my eyes shut for a moment. It was too soon, she still had over a month to go.

"Let me through!"

I'd never been more grateful to hear Donna's voice. The cafe was crawling with my brothers now, everyone getting shit done before the cops made an appearance. I scooped Marie up in my arms and made my way toward Donna, who had Bash helping her push the gurney inside. Fuck, that prospect had earned his patch time and again. If fuckers would quit messing with us, we might get around to voting the kid in. But that was a worry for another day. I laid my woman out on the bed.

"Says she's in labor, but it's too soon."

"We need to get her to the hospital, anyone else need to go?"

I looked around. Tiny had Mercedes sobbing in his arms. And Zara had come to from her attack and Mac was wiping the blood off her face. "Tiny? She good?"

"Nothing I can't handle."

"Mac? Does Zara need that stitched?"

"Nah, I've got it. You get Marie where she needs to be, we got this covered here."

"Cindy and I will take Ariel. I'll bring her in later to see you at the hospital."

I winced that I had to leave Ariel behind. This whole situation wasn't going to do her mental state any favors, but right now, Marie and our boy needed my full attention. I knew Nitro and Cindy would take good care of my girl. I clapped Nitro on the shoulder. "Thanks, brother."

Then I was out, helping get Marie into the bus. One of the best things we ever did was kit out this rig as a private ambulance. Even if we did use the fucker way too often lately, today I was definitely grateful we had it.

Ariel
Everybody left.

I might have only turned five last month and was still a kid, but I knew things. One of those things was that I wasn't good enough for anyone to stay. I thought I'd done the right thing. When the men came in with guns, I got baby Cleo and snuck out the back, through the door to Cindy's shop and told her what happened. Wasn't that the right thing to do? Get the baby to safety and tell an adult. Mommy had given me a smile when she'd seen me taking baby Cleo. I hope she wasn't mad at me.

I sniffled back my tears and tried to curl up into a smaller ball. I wanted to go home. Did I still have a home? I wanted my rabbit. Why hadn't I brought him with me? I used to take him everywhere, but lately I hadn't been remembering to grab him when we went out.

"Oh, sweetie. It's gonna be all right."

It wasn't. That was just what adults told kids. Scout and Marie were gone. My mommy and papa had gone, just like my momma had. I knew it was different. Momma had died and gone to heaven. Mommy and Papa were still alive—at least I thought they were. They just weren't here. They'd left without me. Without telling me why or where they were going. They'd never done that before.

Cindy reached for me but I pulled back. I didn't want to be touched. Didn't want someone else to make me like them, only to vanish on me too. Plus, she was holding baby Cleo, I didn't want her to get hurt because of me.

"Nitro, what do we do? We can't leave her like this. Poor little munchkin."

The big man stood tall, frowning down at me. Would he be like some of the men that Momma and me had lived with? Was he going to hurt me because I didn't do something he wanted me to? Or was he going to be like the ones who just ignored me, pretending like I didn't exist.

"Not sure, Cin. Doesn't help she doesn't know us real well. Here, let me take Cleo and you ring Donna. She should be done with Marie by now and know what to do with Ariel."

I sniffled again as they passed the baby between them. I was jealous of her. I didn't want to be, but I wished I could be like Cleo. Happy to go to Nitro, trusting him. Her baby hands smacked at his face as she spoke words that made no sense at all. The moment Cindy started speaking into her phone, I blocked out everything else and zeroed my attention in on her, trying to find out what was going on. Were they deciding how to send me away?

My heart thudded inside me, almost too loud for me to hear over it. I rubbed my hand over the ache, trying to soothe it like Mommy did her belly when the baby in there started kicking her from the inside. But it didn't work. It still hurt. Was that why they left me? They had their own baby now so they didn't need me anymore?

I sniffled again, trying hard not to cry. No one likes a crybaby. That was something else those mean men had taught me. No one liked having to deal with tears.

Wiping my eyes on my shirt, I blinked up and jerked back when Cindy was only a little way away from me on the floor. She'd crawled in behind the rack of clothes where I'd tried to hide from them all earlier.

"Sweetie, can you come over to me? I'm not going to hurt you and I want to tell you what's happening with your mommy."

I shook my head. I didn't want to move. I liked being in this corner, in the dark.

"Alrighty then, guess I'm coming to you."

Shocked that an adult would do what she was doing, I held my breath as she got closer to me, waiting for her to lash out or maybe grab me to drag me out, but she didn't. She just crawled in and curled up next to me.

"I know you're scared, sweetie. What happened was really awful. But you were so brave. Getting Cleo like you did, and bringing her here? That was the perfect thing to do. Because of what you did, I could call in your papa and he came with the others and stopped the bad men before they could hurt anyone."

I cleared my throat and sniffled again. "Then why'd they leave me? If I did good."

"Oh, sweetie. That's not why they left without you. When the bad men came in with the guns, your mommy got a shock and that upset the baby. Enough that the baby thought he might like to be born early, so she had to go to the hospital so they could convince him to stay inside your mommy for a little bit longer. Your papa went with her to help get her there faster. The only reason they didn't come say goodbye first was that they had to rush to get there. They're not abandoning you at all, Ariel. They'll always be there for you, we all will."

This time when she reached for me, I went to her, moving until I was curled up in her lap. She stroked her hands through my hair and it felt so nice, I started to relax and tangled my hand in the long necklace she wore.

"We'll just sit here for a little while, then we'll take you up to the hospital so you can see them, okay?"

"Uh huh."

They hadn't left me. I wasn't being sent away.

Taking a deep breath, I closed my eyes and pressed my ear to her chest so I could hear her heartbeat as she kept stroking my hair.

Chapter 4

Marie

Staring at the IV in my arm, my thoughts swirled while my stomach churned. The drugs they'd given me had stopped the contractions before I'd gone too far into labor but I would now have to spend the remainder of my pregnancy in the hospital on bed rest. All the while getting fed drugs to speed up my boy's growth because apparently, my baby boy was coming early.

Another chime on Scout's phone had me lifting my gaze to him. He paced the room, running his hands through his hair. I didn't doubt he was wishing he still wore the bandana he used to always wear and constantly adjust. I was grateful when he'd ditched it after he'd discovered I liked to run my fingers through his hair, which I couldn't do if he had that dirty old thing on. Right now it wasn't an old piece of cloth that was bugging me, it was his phone that was constantly going off. He seemed unaware of it, which was impossible with how often the thing was dinging.

"Babe? You gonna check that?"

He jolted, like he'd been in a trance or something, then rushed to my side. "Sorry, what? Where does it hurt? What do you need?"

I reached up and stroked my fingers over his cheek and through his beard as I smiled up at my man. He was a gorgeous beast. I knew he'd move heaven and earth to keep me safe and the fact someone got to me today was killing him inside. We'd only been together for a short time but I'd known this man for over two decades. I knew him. Knew that he wanted to be out there dealing with this threat to us, rather than being stuck in a hospital room, unable to do a damn thing. And to be honest, I could use a little alone time to process.

"Everything will be fine, babe. The doctor has it handled as much as he can. I'm in the best place I can be. And even if our son comes today, it's only a little early. Babies born at thirty-three weeks have a ninety-eight percent chance of survival, at thirty-four weeks, it's ninety-nine percent. He's gonna be fine. So, please, for all our sakes, answer your damn phone before whoever it is blowing it up decides to come in here to yell at you for not answering the damn thing."

With a chuckle and a shake of his head, he leaned in and kissed me before standing up straight.

"No idea how you know that shit off the top of your head, babe. And if I see any one of the texts coming in, I'll have to go deal with whatever it is about. I don't want to leave you."

I didn't want to tell him how much Googling I'd been doing since becoming pregnant. I didn't want to give him ideas.

"How about you just have a quick look to see if there's anything about Ariel?"

His jaw clenched for a split second before he had his phone out and unlocked. With everything that had happened, our poor little angel had to be struggling. Back at the cafe, I'd heard Nitro say he and Cindy would take her, so I knew she was safe, but I wasn't so sure about how she'd be coping mentally with what happened today. We didn't have time to tell her where we were going, or that we were coming back. Since Sarah's death, Ariel had issues with people leaving. Poor little love was simply too young to understand everything that had happened in her life. Really, she did quite well but there were a few things she didn't handle easily, and not knowing where Scout and I were and when we were going to return was one of them.

"Ah, shit."

Before I could ask what was going on, he had the phone to his ear.

"Hey, Nitro. Got your message. Marie's doing good, they stopped the labor for now. How's my girl?"

Lifting my hand I chewed on my thumbnail when Scout winced and rubbed his eyes.

"Fuck. Yeah, bring her in. We're in room three in the maternity ward."

He ended the call and came back to sit in the chair next to the bed.

"Ariel freaked the fuck out. Thought we'd abandoned her. Fuck. I didn't even think to stop for a minute and explain what was going on to her."

I reached out and took his hand in mine. "Neither of us did, Charlie. And honestly, we didn't have the time. Baby boy wanted out and we needed to get here as quickly as possible. We're about to add another child to our family, there are going to be times when one needs our attention over the other. This isn't going to be the last time this happens. We just need to make sure Ariel understands we love her and nothing is going to change that, nothing is ever going to make us abandon her."

My man looked so lost, like he'd failed somehow. I was feeling a little the same way, despite what I'd just told him.

"She crawled in behind a clothing rack and curled up in the shadows. Wouldn't come out to Cindy. Woman had to go in after her."

My eyes stung at both Ariel's level of distress and how beautiful Cindy was for putting the effort in to go crawling in behind racks for our daughter. Releasing his hand, I cupped his face, turning him until his gaze was on mine.

"Babe, she's going to be just fine. I hope Cindy managed to get through to her. Once she gets more confident in her place with us, she'll realize she has the whole Charon family at her back. That she won't ever be left alone. She just needs some more time, you'll see."

He leaned in and kissed me, holding my face in his palms as he made love to my mouth with his. When he pulled back, I was a little breathless. But I wasn't stressing about the baby or Ariel anymore. Nope, I was thinking maybe he could go lock the door and come back here.

"Love you so fucking much, Marie. Today scared the hell out of me."

And just like that, all thoughts of locking the door fled. Today had terrified me. For as long as I lived, I would never forget how it felt to have a gun muzzle pressed up against my stomach, against my unborn child.

"Who does that? Threaten an unborn baby? I was so scared, Charlie. I knew you'd come for us, but I had no idea how quickly."

I blinked back tears.

"I will always come for you, Marie. Always."

"I love you."

His gaze softened at my words, then he leaned in and kissed me again, only pulling away when the door opened and Nitro's laugh echoed around the room.

"I'd tell you two to get a room, but you already have one."

"Shut up, already."

Scout was already halfway across the room, heading for Cindy, who had Ariel in her arms.

"Hey, sweet angel, I'm sorry we left you like we did, but we had to get to the hospital to make sure your little brother was going to be okay. I knew you'd be safe with Nitro and Cindy. I never would have left you if I hadn't known you'd be safe and well cared for."

My fingers itched with the need to hold my girl. I know technically she was Sarah's daughter, but she was Scout's and mine, too. And the little boy in my belly would be her baby brother.

Her sniffle was loud in the room and she continued to cling to Cindy for a few seconds before lifting her face to look toward first Scout, then over to me. The color drained from her face as her eyes peeled wide. Of course she'd panic at seeing me like this. In a hospital bed, just like her mother before she'd died.

"I'm fine, Ariel. I'm going to be perfectly okay. All these machines are just to keep track of your brother's heartbeat and mine. Looks like he's a little impatient and wants to be born early."

Cindy handed her over to Scout, who cuddled her close as he strode over toward me. Times like this it was handy she was so small for her age. She fit in Scout's arms perfectly.

"That's right, we're all okay. No one's going anywhere, Ariel."

Scout tried to sit down with her but she twisted around, reaching for me. I carefully shifted over on the bed, making as much room as I could for her.

"Hold on, angel, let me help you."

He placed her next to me on the bed and she instantly clung to me.

"I'm so sorry we scared you, sweet girl. You were so brave this morning. You saved Cleo and yourself—then by telling Cindy, you saved me, Zara and Mercedes. I'm so very proud of you."

"We all are, Ariel. Everyone is extremely grateful for what you did today."

I wrapped my arm around her and with a sniffle, she cuddled in against me, relaxing when she closed her eyes and drifted off. Poor kid had had a rough damn day so far.

Scout

Hearing my phone chime again, I knew I couldn't put off dealing with the Ice Rider bullshit any longer. I didn't want to leave. Marie was being overly calm but I knew there was a storm brewing under her surface. She clearly didn't want to discuss it yet, so I'd leave her be for now. I ran my gaze over both my girls as I stood.

"Unfortunately, I've gotta head out and deal with all this shit. I'll be back later. Do you want me to take Ariel with me?"

I wasn't sure what the fuck I'd do with her if she did come with me, but if Marie needed a little alone time, I'd work something out.

"Nah, leave her here. She'll probably sleep for a while. She's had a rough morning."

With a nod, I pressed a kiss to Ariel's head before pressing my lips to Marie's.

"Love you, babe."

"Love you too, Scout. Stay safe."

"Always."

It'd be so much easier to keep myself and everyone else safe if these bastards would quit coming after us. I followed Nitro and Cindy out of the room and toward the front entrance.

"Your bike's back at the clubhouse, I'll take you back there. Just need to drop Cindy off at the shop on our way."

"Good deal."

As he drove, I went through my phone, checking all the messages that had rolled in while I'd been with Marie. I responded to Bulldog, saying I was on my way in with Nitro. The others were mainly everyone wanting an update on Marie and the baby, so I shot off a group text to them all, letting them know the drill. Then I sat back and, taking a deep breath, attempted to push all the personal stuff aside. I needed to be the president of the Charon MC when I walked into the clubhouse, not the concerned husband and father who'd thought his world was going to end earlier this morning.

I gave Cindy a nod goodbye when she hopped from the cage, then we were off to the clubhouse.

"Cin did a good job on that fucker. Tank, the one she hit, hasn't woken up since. Taz doesn't think he will. His jaw is fucked from the bat and he shattered his nose on the table when he went down."

I still couldn't believe Cindy pulled that shit. I huffed out a laugh. "Remind me not to fuck with your woman. Damn."

"What can I say? Roller derby girls kick ass."

Apparently they did.

"What about the other guy? Rumble. He talking?"

"No one's tried talking to him yet. But he is at least conscious. Taz patched up his shoulder from Mac's bullet, then we tossed him down into the cell to wait for you. Figured you'd want the pleasure of dealing with him."

"You put them together?"

"Nah, kept them separate. Figured you could use Tank against Rumble if he doesn't know his buddy's already as good as dead."

I nodded. "Yeah. Guess Mac and Tiny are gonna want front row seats for dealing with these fuckers."

"Yeah. Mercedes took it hard, poor girl. I think Tiny's still with her up in their room at the clubhouse. Hopefully, she'll snap out of it soon."

Mercedes was a lot like Ariel. Raised within a fucking cult, she had warped concepts of how the world worked. But unlike Ariel, Mercedes was a grown fucking woman so had the maturity to understand more. She also had Tiny, who worshiped the fucking ground she walked on.

I knew she'd be fine, it might just take a little while to get her there.

"Tiny'll get her sorted."

We pulled up and I glanced at the lineup of bikes, happy to see mine at the front of them, shiny and sparkling in the sun. Prospects were doing good, keeping our rides clean. Feeling the heat of the Texas summer sun had me looking up at the sky for a moment after I got out of the vehicle.

"How the fuck has so much shit happened already today? It's barely past lunch time, for fuck's sake."

"Tell me about it, brother."

He clapped me on the shoulder and we both made our way inside. Bulldog was waiting for me at the bar, shoving a glass in my hand before I could say a word. "Fucker can wait another ten minutes while you take a breath, brother."

He was right, of course, and after draining the whiskey in one go, I slid onto the stool beside him and knocked the empty glass on the bar. Keg was fast on the refill and I took another mouthful before Bulldog spoke again.

"Marie and the baby doing okay now?"

I ran a hand through my hair, missing my bandana as I sighed.

"Technically, yes. Doc said they're just holding off labor for as long as they can to give my boy the best chance of survival. He's going to be born early, no question. Doc's hoping they can hold the birth off for at least a week so they can keep Marie on the drugs to speed up his lung development and other shit. I can tell Marie's already hating this whole bed rest thing. But because she's high risk, they don't want her going home and possibly going into labor again."

Bulldog nodded. "Sounds like the hospital is the best place for her. Because, brother, we both know that woman wouldn't rest up if she were at home."

I tossed back my second drink, enjoying the burn. "Ain't that the truth? Okay. Let's go see if we can get this fucker to sing. Figure out what the fuck we're dealing with. Wanna grab Tiny and Mac for me? I assume they're both here somewhere."

"I'll head up and grab them."

I gave Nitro a nod and he jogged up the stairs.

"Zara's doing okay. Mac's got her and Cleo up in his room. She took her meds, so she'll be fine on her own with Cleo. Hopefully Tiny's gotten Mercedes to take the sleeping pill Donna gave him for her. Guessing the shit this morning hit all sorts of triggers for her."

I nodded to Keg. Like Bash, he'd earned his top rocker time and again, but we hadn't had the time to bring it to church to vote either of them in. Thinking about the club's women, I shook my head. Even our women had demons. But that was okay, the Charon MC was family and we took care of our own, no matter how big the demon they had biting at their heels.

Certain Mac and Tiny weren't far away, I rose from my stool and started toward the back, where the hidden stairs were located. I wasn't sure Rumble would have anything new to tell me, considering the fact he didn't seem to have known much when he spoke earlier, but it was worth a shot. And fuck, I had some stress to work out and there was nothing better than tormenting an asshole who'd come after what was mine to relieve it.

By the time I hit the bottom of the stairs, Bulldog, Mac and Tiny had joined me.

"Your women doing okay?"

Tiny nodded. "Yeah, got her to take the pill Donna gave me, so she's thankfully fast asleep. She's torn up because she didn't do anything to help. She froze in panic and couldn't act. It brought back the shit that happened with her mom. She'll be fine. I'll make sure of it."

"Zara's good. She cut her face when she fell against a chair, but it looked worse than it was. Didn't even need stitches. She's taken her meds and is her usual self now. Well, she's worrying herself sick over Marie and the baby, but aside from that, she's good."

I was relieved to hear that they'd both made it out of the morning without any long-term effects.

"Excellent. Let her know Marie's doing okay. Our boy's going to be coming early, but the doc's got the labor stopped for now. Why don't you take Zara in to see her later? Ease both their minds, since I know Marie's worried about her, too." I paused to blow out a breath. "Okay, let's get this shit done with so we can all go back to our women, yeah?"

I couldn't help but smirk at the way Tiny cracked his knuckles while Mac rolled his neck. Yep, they were with me on this one. This fucker messed with the wrong damn club.

Bulldog unlocked the door, and I slammed it open hard and fast, the sound of the thing hitting the wall echoing loudly around us. I took three steps in, then stood staring at the piece of shit tied to a chair in front of me. He didn't look so tough now, not stripped down to his jeans. The red bleeding through the center of the white bandage Taz had put over his wounded shoulder stood out against his skin.

"Just in case you forgot who the fuck I am, I'm the motherfucking president of the Charon MC. And it was my pregnant old lady you threatened this morning. Sent her into early fucking labor with your bullshit. So, I'd recommend not testing me anymore and just answer my fucking questions because I'm all out of patience for your shit."

"Or what? I'm not a fool. I know I ain't walking out of here no matter what I say, or don't say. So why would I give you a fucking thing?"

"More than one way to kill a man. Mac, here, served a few tours in the Middle East, learned some things. And it was his old lady who you left bleeding on the fucking floor this morning-"

His face paled. "No one was supposed to get hurt. The plan was to just hold the women, so when we called, you'd take us seriously."

Tiny moved to stand behind him, wrapping a hand around his injured shoulder, squeezing the bullet wound. "Yeah? How'd that work out for you?"

"Enough." Tiny released his grip at my command and Rumble groaned as his body sagged in the chair. "Who are you, exactly, and why'd you come into my town?"

"I'm an enforcer for the Ice Riders MC. My president sent me down here with Tank to get that ledger from you, and anything else of ours you received from John Bennett."

"How'd your president find out about the ledger in the first place?"

"Some mobster from L.A. told him. Club's been having issues with one of the cartels in New York. Chains got word this guy, Sabella, in L.A., might have some dirt we could use on them. Sabella told Chains that when we got our stuff from you, it would include a key to a safe deposit box. As soon as he got that key, he'd give Chains what we need to deal with the cartel."

I turned to Mac. "We need to deal with that fucker once and for all, you hear me?"

Moving his gaze from Rumble to me, he gave me a short nod. "Yeah, I know. I'll start working on it."

The look in his eyes told me that despite him not wanting to have anything to do with those fuckers in L.A. ever again, he'd step up and get it done. Before joining the Marines, Mac had gotten himself tangled up with the mob in L.A. He'd enlisted in the USMC to escape their hold on him. Thanks to his time with them, he had the contacts and the knowledge to pull this shit off. But first, we'd deal with this little Ice Rider problem.

"How many of you came down here?"

"Just us two."

"And how long until you're supposed to check in?"

"Weren't given set times. We were to call in when we had the stuff. Where's Tank?"

I stared at him for a minute, weighing what to do next. I could just kill the fucker now and be done with it, but I might need to ask him more questions, or use him for leverage, later.

"We'll bring him in for you."

With that I spun on my heel and left the room, expecting the other two to follow me. Once the door was shut, Tiny started.

"What the fuck, prez? Why's he still breathing?"

"Calm the fuck down and think. Dead men can't answer questions, and we might still need him. Plus, you don't think letting him sit there watching his brother in a coma, with his face smashed in, not getting any medical aid, is gonna be worse torture than anything we can physically do to him? Save your strength, we're gonna need it for this war that's brewing."

I saw the shudder go through Mac. I wasn't entirely sure what he'd seen when he'd been overseas, but I knew it had left its mark. And hell, he saw with Zara on the daily how much a person's mind could fuck them up.

I opened the door for Mac and Tiny to carry Tank's limp body into the room with Rumble, keeping my gaze on the asshole as he saw what condition his brother was in. The agonized groan he let out was music to my ears. I didn't say another word as my brothers exited the room and I shut the door. Didn't need to. Our message was clear. Fuck with us, we'll fuck you back. Harder.

Once we were back upstairs, I grabbed Bulldog before he could go anywhere.

"Call everyone in for church at five, like we were originally planning. I'll be at the hospital till then."

"On it, prez."

Chapter 5

Ariel

I hated that Mommy was in the hospital, just like Momma had been. Momma died in a big white bed just like the one Mommy was now in. But she and Papa kept telling me that this was different, this was to make sure my little brother was going to be okay. Mommy was fine.

I wasn't sure I could believe them until I heard Momma whisper in my ear that it was real. That she knew for sure that both Marie and the baby would be just fine. I didn't understand how she knew, or how she managed to talk to me from heaven, but Momma had never lied to me. I knew she wouldn't now. Not about something this important.

I wriggled in closer to Mommy, shifting my head so my ear was pressed against her chest. I loved being able to hear her heartbeat. The regular beat of it soothed me whenever I was upset. Right now, I could also hear my little brother's heartbeat, thanks to this neat little machine Mommy had on her tummy. I couldn't wait to meet him and spend lots of time imagining what he'll look like.

Mommy ran her fingers through my hair and I hummed. My mind was still trying to process everything that had happened earlier. After the scary stuff had finished in the cafe, I'd been sure I was being left behind—forgotten—but I'd been wrong. Once I'd given in and gone to Cindy, she'd let me stay on her lap for a long time. She told me stories about her roller derby friends and had promised she'd teach me to skate if I wanted to. I did. Skating sounded like fun, but I wasn't sure I could do what Cindy did. That sounded way too dangerous for me.

Then she and Nitro brought me to Mommy and Papa. They weren't mad at me, like I'd thought they'd be. Instead, they were happy about what I'd done. Told me I'd saved Cleo and everyone else because I did what I did. That made me smile. It was me going for help that saved Mommy, my brother, Zara and Mercedes. I liked making them proud of me. It made me feel warm and happy inside and I wanted to stay right where I was.

"Mommy?"

"Yeah, angel?"

"Can I stay here with you? Until you come home."

"I'm sorry, sweetie—"

I sat up and looked her in the eye, as all the warm fuzzy feelings inside me vanished. She couldn't send me away! "But you said I did good! You can't send me away!"

"Ariel, you need to calm down and let me finish, because it's not that simple. First up, I need you to understand that we will never send you away. It's not dependent on your being good or bad, or anything else. I know you're scared of something happening that'll leave you alone, but that won't ever happen. We love you and you're part of our family. That family includes all the men and women in the Charon MC. You'll never ever be left all alone again. So I need you to stop thinking we're throwing you away every time something separates one of us from you, okay?"

Despite the fact my heart was still beating hard in my chest, I nodded. Not because I believed her, but because I wanted to hear what else she was going to say.

"What happened this morning in the cafe put a lot of stress on my body. Sometimes, when that happens to a woman who's heavily pregnant, the baby decides they want out early. But it's still a little early for him to be born. The doctors have given me medicine that has stopped him for now. But they're worried if I go home, it'll happen again and either he or I could get hurt. So, the doctors are keeping me here in the hospital until he's born. Ariel, this room just isn't big enough for you and Scout to stay here too. That means you need to go home with Scout each day, that way you'll get to sleep in your own bed. And I promise, every day he'll bring you in to visit me, okay?"

I'd listened carefully to every word Mommy had said. I understood she wanted me to go with Papa at night, and I could spend my days with her here.

I could live with that.

They weren't leaving me.

I wasn't going to be left on my own.

Scout

I hit the gavel on the table to call church to order. Bulldog had done well and had managed to get hold of basically everyone. There were a few missing, but brothers had jobs and families. Two were still serving overseas. Life happened, sometimes you couldn't make it in. We all understood and accepted that. And Bulldog would make sure all those missing would be brought up to speed as soon as he could.

"Everyone shut the fuck up already, I've got places I need to be."

Like with my wife and kids. I did not have the time or patience for bullshit today.

Within seconds I had silence, proving my brothers' were smart men.

"Y'all were here when shit went down with the L.A. mob two years back, but I'll give you a quick refresher. Silk's dad, John Bennett was a piece of shit who's still fucking haunting us from beyond the grave. Bastard kept ledgers of not just financial information, but locations and details of other stuff. Idiot also stole who knows how much money from the mob. No clue if he did the same with the other organizations he kept dirt on. Sabella, the head of the L.A. mob, was the only one who figured out what John was doing before his death. When John died in the 9/11 attacks, Sabella assumed the ledgers went with him, along with all traces of the cash he'd stolen. Two years ago, it was discovered John's bag missed the flight and was still at LAX. When Silk got her father's bag, it didn't have just one ledger but six. L.A. mob, N.Y. mob, Satan's Knights MC, Iron Hammers MC, Ice Riders MC and us. The L.A. one was the first we dealt with, handing it over to Sabella in order for him to leave Silk the fuck alone. That ledger had a key to a safety deposit box in it. That box had cash and a copy of the ledger in it. Obviously, it wasn't all the cash he'd stolen and it looks like Sabella is now trying to get his hands on the other boxes and the rest of his cash. Somehow the fucker figured out John had a book on the Ice Riders, so he sent them down here to collect it." I paused to scrub a hand over my face before continuing.

"From what we know, the Ice Riders MC up in Boston got themselves in trouble with a cartel in New York. They went looking for dirt to use against the cartel and found Sabella, who told them about the ledger. Spun some bullshit that we were planning on heading up there to do fuck knows what, so they sent their boys down here to collect their ledger along with the key inside the thing. He told them if they hand the key over to him, in return he'd give them the dirt they need to deal with their cartel trouble."

I glanced around the room at my brothers before continuing.

"Which leads us to what happened this morning. Two of the Ice Riders enforcers stormed Marie's Cafe. They let the customers flee, but held Marie, Zara and Mercedes at fucking gunpoint. They held a fucking gun on my woman, against her belly. Threatened my unborn son."

My voice was a growl that echoed around the room. Rage coursed through me and I clenched my fists as I closed my eyes and tried to get a handle on it. Nitro stepped up to take over for me, for which I was grateful.

"The kids were there, too. Ariel and Cleo were both in the cafe. Ariel did us proud. Before the Riders even noticed they were there, Ariel had Cleo free of the play-pen and out the back door. She went through to Retro Funk and told Cindy what was going on. She called us in, and because of the early warning we got there and ended shit before things got ugly."

He paused to look to me and I gave him a nod that I was good to take back over.

"Zara had an attack and hit her head when she fell, but she'll be fine. It fucked with Mercedes' head some but Tiny'll make sure she gets back on track. The stress of it all sent Marie into early labor. We got her to hospital in time for them to stop it, but the Doc says my boy's coming early. Marie's gonna have to stay in hospital until he's born and well, basically, they're just trying to keep him inside for as long as they can while they pump Marie with drugs to make sure his lungs and other organs are fully developed in time." I scrubbed my face again, wishing this shit was over with already, so I could get back to her. I hated having to leave her side at all right now.

"We have the two Riders downstairs and they'll obviously be dealt with, along with the rest of their fucking club. We also need to find a way to shut down Sabella and his shit permanently. I'm open to suggestions."

Mac lifted his hand and I gave him a nod to go ahead.

"Do you know which cartel they're having issues with? If it's one that's linked to whichever family the ledger is about, we could use that and get them to help us deal with them."

I stroked my beard for a minute, thinking it over before I responded.

"I don't know, but we can ask the boys downstairs if we need to. But I'm not sure getting mixed up with a mob family or cartel is a good idea. Once they get their claws into a club, it's hard to get the fuckers back out. But you got me thinking. There were a few guys I met a while back on a run we did with the BACA. Actually, we've done a few runs with them in the last few years and—"

Bulldog snickered and I shot him a glare.

"Oh, c'mon, brother. I know who you're talking about, I've been on runs with them too, remember?"

I rubbed my eyes. "Wolf and I do not look like we're fucking brothers. Yeah, we both have beards—"

"You don't look like brothers, Scout, you look like fucking twins."

I glared at my VP again. "Says the man who shares a name with one of them. *Bulldog.*"

Bastard just grinned at me, so I cleared my throat and got back on track. "Anyway, as I was saying before this fucking clown interrupted me—these men are from a club up in New York, the Satan's Knights. I've spoken with their president, Parrish, a few times and he told me if we ever needed their help, to just give him a call."

Arrow spoke up. "I spoke to a few of their guys on those runs too. They're solid—fucking nuts—but solid guys. And I agree with Scout, I'd prefer deal with another MC than a fucking cartel. I think it's worth making a call or two."

I gave him a nod. "I'll put a call in to Parrish once we're done here. Mac, you, Tiny and Taz head down and ask that fucker if he knows the name of the cartel. Then I want you to go over those ledgers for Ice Riders and the N.Y. mob. I want you to know those fucking things by heart. You hear me?"

"Crystal clear, prez. I'll get on it as soon as we finish here."

"Come with me once we're done, and I'll get them out of the safe for you. They don't leave the clubhouse, understand?"

"Yes, prez."

"Right. Fucker told us it was just him and his buddy who came down here, but I don't trust him, so keep your eyes and ears open and report back anything you notice. Nitro, sort the prospects out on protection detail for the women and our businesses. Not having a fucking repeat of this morning go down."

"On it."

"Great, then we're done. We'll have church again Friday as usual and see where we are then."

With that, I cracked the gavel on the table then stood, more than ready to get back to my woman. Not that I could, just yet. I grabbed my phone from the locker and made my way to my office with Mac beside me. I made fast work of opening up the safe and retrieving the correct books before handing them over to Mac.

"When you're done, find Bulldog, Keys, Arrow or Nitro to lock 'em back up again. I don't want them to be left unattended at any time. Got me?"

"Yes, prez. I got it."

After closing up the safe, I went and sat at my desk while Mac headed off. Once alone, I pulled my phone out, praying Parrish would be able to help us out. In the back of my mind I knew we'd have to send at least a few Charons up north, but I didn't want to leave Marie while she was in the hospital. I definitely didn't want to fucking miss the birth of my boy. I'd given this club my all for so long, surely, I was entitled to a few fucking weeks off to spend with my family.

Pulling up Parrish's contact details, I hit dial and lifted the phone to my ear. Then cursed when it went through to voicemail. Ending the call, I dropped my phone to the desk then scrubbed my hands over my face as my thoughts continued to race. A knock on the door had me dropping my hands down and looking towards the sound.

"Hey, brother."

Arrow came in and grabbed a bottle and two glasses before he sat down, placing everything on the desk between us before pouring a healthy serving of whiskey in them both. He took one and cocked his eyebrow at me until I reached for the other one. He waited until I took a swig before he spoke.

"When the time comes to head up north, I'll take the lead. You need to stay here right now."

I gave him a nod and took another mouthful before answering him. Normally a VP would go in the president's place, but we both knew that wasn't going to happen this time. "Bulldog's arthritis is getting worse. He's spoken to me about stepping down as VP. He doesn't feel he can do the role justice with his health issues."

Which fucking sucked. Bulldog had been my best friend and right hand for more years than I could count. I hated I couldn't keep him by my side as VP, but we both understood an MC was a team. A machine that needed all its parts in order to function correctly. Arrow's gaze didn't miss a thing, and he had a sharp mind. So I wasn't surprised when he read between the lines of what I wasn't saying. "You already got someone in mind, don't you?"

I nodded. "Yep. When the time comes to go north, it'll be you and Mac taking the lead. I want you to watch him, throw things his way to see what he does."

"You want me to test him? He'll pass, I'm sure of it. He's a good choice. He's level-headed, cool under pressure. And he's a fucking Marine so you know he can handle himself in just about any situation."

I finished off my drink. "Yep. I'd happily have him at my back any day. But we need to be sure, so dealing with the Ice Riders, then Sabella, will be his test. Once that shit's all dealt with, we'll vote him in."

"Got a few prospects due to be patched in too, prez. I know we've had a lot of shit go down lately, but those boys have earned their top rockers time and again. They're due."

I nodded again. "Yeah, I know. Bash especially, but Keg and Jazz need to be patched in too. We'll handle it all after this shit is done with. Have a big blow-out and celebrate in style."

Chapter 6

Scout

My phone ringing woke me up way too early. With a groan I rolled over and snatched it off the table, wincing when I saw the clock. It was only six am. I'd slept like shit these past two nights without Marie beside me, but I couldn't stay at the hospital. I had Ariel to take care of, as well as the club. Now my day had started before I was ready, and I knew this call from Tiny would be more bad news, meaning I would be in for another long, fucking day.

"What's happened?"

"Tank went to meet his maker and Rumble ain't happy about it. We need to deal with him."

Fuck me. Just what I needed. "Yeah, he ain't gonna tell us anything else. I'll be there in twenty. Just shut the door and head upstairs. It's soundproof so no one's gonna hear him hollering. I'll call Mac and bring him in with me. He'll want to be there."

Ending the call, I rolled out of bed and headed to the bathroom. After taking a piss and splashing some cold water over my face, I headed out to get dressed. There was no time for a shower, not that it mattered since I was pretty sure I was gonna need one later, anyhow.

Snatching up my phone, I dialed Mac.

"Hey prez. What's happening?"

"We need to get to the clubhouse. I'll pick you up in ten. Can Zara drop Ariel in to Marie at the hospital for me?"

"Let me check."

Speaking of Ariel, where was she? Even with Marie not here, she'd come in the past two mornings to say good morning and have a quick cuddle. While waiting for Mac, I headed down to her bedroom. My heart rate kicked up when I found it empty.

"Ariel?"

I quickly looked under the bed and in the closet, but she wasn't there. Forgetting about Mac, I ran through the house, looking in every room and calling out her name. Where the fuck was she? Skidding into the kitchen I saw the back door had been left open.

"Scout!"

The tinny voice coming from my phone had me lifting it back up to my ear.

"Ariel's gone."

"I'm on my way."

Hanging up, I slipped the phone in my pocket and headed out the open doorway. Over the past couple years, a number of us had all bought homes on the same street. I knew I'd have Mac, Taz and Eagle, along with all their women, here within minutes. If Tiny wasn't at the clubhouse, he would be here too. As I waited for them, I scoured the back yard, calling her name as I looked in every hiding spot I could think of. Where was she? And why the fuck had she run?

Or had she been taken?

Ice flowed through my veins at the thought. Ariel had already been through more than enough in her short life. If some fucker had touched my girl, I was going to end them in the slowest, most painful way possible.

I was standing at the rear of my yard, staring at the wildness that was beyond the low fence when Mac came up beside me.

"I spoke with Tiny. He visited Rumble and says that he vows there were only the two of them who came down here. I don't think someone snatched her, prez. If they had, and left a door open, it would be the front door, not the back. And I'm pretty sure she'd put up a fight if someone tried to take her. She might be little, but she's been hanging around with our girls long enough to pick up a few things. Nothing inside looks disturbed."

I nodded. I'd had the same thoughts. "She ran away. Why the fuck did she run? And where would she go?" Poor kid had no one else. "Need to call the cops in. We need to start searching for her. She's too young to be out there on her own."

"Eagle's already on it. They're on their way."

My eyes stung but I shoved the emotion aside, "I'm gonna have to tell Marie." She may never forgive me.

She gave me one fucking job to do while she was in hospital. Take care of our girl.

"Stop. You can let your guilt reign later. Right now, we need to focus on finding her."

I nodded, knowing he was right but still unable to push it aside completely. What had happened to send her running? I followed Mac to the house where several of my brothers were now standing around waiting for my orders. But I had no idea what to say, where to start. Ariel wasn't mine by virtue of blood, but she was my fucking daughter in my heart and soul. I'd do anything for the kid and right now I didn't know where she was, what had sent her running. It was tearing me up, and I didn't know what the fuck to do about it.

Ariel

Rubbing the tears from my eyes, I kept walking. I'd heard Papa on the phone, saying he'd be somewhere in twenty minutes. Just him. Not me. He didn't say "we'd" be there, just that he would. I knew with Mommy in hospital, he was worried. Not as happy as he usually was when Mommy was home. And he was needed by his club. I wasn't exactly sure what he did for it, but I thought he might the boss there. Everyone always asked him for orders. In some ways the club reminded me of where I lived with Momma. Although, there were more women and kids here. And the men didn't appear to be as mean as Bruce's men.

It always seemed like people always needed him. He didn't have time for me. Not time to sing to me after he tucked me in, like Mommy normally did, or to stay in bed until I came to give him a cuddle. I'd tried this morning, just like I had yesterday but he'd already been sitting on the edge of the bed, talking on his phone about needing to be somewhere. I'd heard every word he'd said and not one of them was about me. He'd forgotten I was there and he needed to go in twenty minutes.

I don't need him. I can take care of myself.

Momma had told me time and again how the only one you could ever truly count on was yourself. She'd told me I could count on her, but if she wasn't around anymore I needed to rely on myself. I wasn't entirely sure what she'd meant, but today Scout upset me and it was time to leave for a while.

With a sniffle, I wiped my eyes again. I missed Momma. Before she'd died, I'd never been away from her for more than a few hours. It had been months since I'd seen her. The times she'd visit me from heaven and whisper in my ear made me feel very good. I wished she'd do it more often, but I guess she was busy up there.

Walking around another clump of trees, I was at the side of a road with houses up one side and nothing but grass and trees on the other. With a frown I looked around, trying to work out where I was as I kept walking.

I wanted to go visit Momma, I just needed to remember the way.

Scout

It was about an hour after I'd noticed Ariel was missing when Keys strolled through my front door with his open laptop balanced on his palm.

"Got her."

I stopped my pacing and turned to face him. I'd been forced to stay here with a damn cop while everyone else was out searching the woods for my girl.

"How?" I shook my head. "Scratch that, I don't give a shit. Where? Where's my girl?"

"Guessing she went to visit her momma. She's at the cemetery. C'mon, I'll drive."

I told the cop that we've got it covered and I'd call it in if she wasn't there. He wasn't happy but knew a brick wall when he saw one, so didn't argue as he cursed and headed to his patrol car. The moment we were in Keys' cage, he shut his laptop and tossed it on the backseat.

"How?"

He smirked over at me. "How'd you think?"

"She doesn't have a fucking phone or car, brother. How'd you lo-jack her?"

"Shoes, a few of her favorite toys. Also her bag, but she didn't take that with her. I've tagged all sorts of her shit just in case anything ever happened."

Keys was a paranoid bastard, but it paid off at times. "Good man. Keep that shit up."

"Didn't plan on stopping, prez."

We rolled up to the cemetery and Keys parked out the front rather than going inside and giving us away.

"I think you need to handle this one on your own, Scout. I'll stay out here and wait for you."

He was right. Whatever had sent her running, I needed to deal with. Me. On my own, because this time Marie wasn't here to do it for me.

"Thanks, man. I won't be too long." *Hopefully.*

Leaving the car, I headed up the path toward where we'd laid Sarah to rest last December, praying Ariel was still there. I didn't doubt Keys had put trackers on her stuff, but she could have moved on since Keys had last checked her location.

Bridgewater Cemetery wasn't huge, so it thankfully didn't take long for me to spot Sarah's tombstone and the little girl sitting in front of it. She had the dolls Sarah made for her, using both her own hair along with Ariel's for the toys. Ariel sat stroking that last piece of her mother she had left and her lips were moving as she spoke with her momma. I couldn't hear her words, but she was clearly totally engrossed in the conversation she was having. Guilt hit me hard, square in the chest. We hadn't brought her back here more than a few times since the funeral. Honestly, I hadn't realized it was something she'd want to do. But what I was watching right now proved how wrong we'd been. As soon as I got done with all this Ice Rider shit today, I'd go visit with Marie and talk to her about setting up a routine of bringing Ariel here to visit more regularly. Maybe once a week, so she could have some time with her mother.

I scrubbed my hand over my hair as I strode toward her. I was still so fresh to this whole parent thing. I didn't have time to wrap my head around becoming a dad before Ariel landed in our laps, making it a reality in an instant. Every day I did my best to nail this dad thing, but some days, like today, I felt like I was fucking drowning, failing at it. Marie seemed to be handling it all so much better than me. She took to motherhood like a duck to water, just as I knew she would. But she wasn't here now. Nope, she was stuck in the hospital. I winced at that thought of having to tell her about this shit. She didn't even know Ariel had gone missing. I hadn't wanted to stress her out with it since she couldn't do anything to help find her. I'd tell her later, after I took Ariel in to see her. She was gonna be angry I didn't tell her as soon as I realized she was missing, but hopefully she'd understand my reasons and forgive me since she was now found and safe.

As I got closer, the gravel crunched under my shoes and Ariel lifted her head and her hazel eyes grew wide as her mouth dropped open. Before I said a word, I dropped down to sit beside her, getting down to her level.

"Hey, sweet angel. Been worried about you."

Her grip tightened on her dolls and her shoulders rolled in, as she tried to make herself smaller.

"It's okay, Ariel. Take some deep breaths and settle down. You're not in trouble. I'm not mad. I was worried when I couldn't find you this morning."

I wanted to ask her why she'd run off, but she still didn't talk all that much to me. I understood it. That fucked up place she was raised in had been mostly men and her mother had, rightfully, taught her not to trust any of them. Instead, I nodded toward Sarah's headstone.

"I didn't know you wanted to come visit your momma. I would have brought you, angel. If you ever want to come here, all you gotta do is ask us. But you can't just run off like today. Scared the hell out of me when I couldn't find you. Got the whole club out looking for you. You have a whole lot of people who care about you now. You're not alone anymore, Ariel. I know you're young, and I'm probably using words you don't understand, but I'm not sure how else to tell you."

Hanging my head down, I rubbed my eyes. I seriously had no clue what to do or say right now. Fuck, I should have told Marie. At least then I could have had her on speaker phone or something. Hearing her move, I cracked my eyes open to see what she was up to. She was shifting and moving toward me. I stayed still, barely breathing, waiting to see what she had planned. It was rare for Ariel to come to me like this, she naturally gravitated toward women. I understood why, but it still hurt when she'd so willingly give Marie affection but not me. I loved this kid as if she were my own.

When she put her palm on my shoulder to balance herself as she moved into my lap I shifted around to give her room. When she curled up against my chest, her ear pressed up against my heart, I wrapped my arms around her, holding her little body against me.

"I'm sorry, Papa. You needed to go out so I thought I'd come here and be out of the way."

I winced again as I heard what she wasn't saying. She'd heard me say I needed to be somewhere and thought I'd forgotten about her. I stroked a palm over her hair, before pressing a kiss to the top of her head.

"You came into the bedroom this morning and heard me on the phone, didn't you, sweetheart? I made a call after that one that I think you missed. I called Mac. Zara and Cleo were on their way over to pick you up to go visit Mommy. I hadn't forgotten you, Ariel. I'll *never* forget you. My job with the club means that sometimes I do have to drop things and go deal with sh—issues." I was trying to not swear around her, but damn it was hard. "But I'll never not take care of you first. Do you understand?"

"Yes, Papa. Can we go visit Mommy now? Or do you still need to go?"

Fuck me. We really needed to work on this girl's self-esteem.

"I think going to see Mommy is a great idea. The club stuff can wait. You're more important. And maybe later, after I come pick you up from the hospital, we can get some flowers and bring them back here for Momma? Maybe some sunflowers? Sound good?"

Marie had let her pick a flower to put on the coffin, and she'd picked the biggest sunflower the shop had.

"Oh, yes."

I stood with her in my arms and she happily snuggled in against me, melting my heart toward her even more as I walked back toward where Keys was waiting for us.

Chapter 7

Marie

By the time Scout strolled through the door with Ariel, I was about ready to come out of my skin. They were late. Like they arrived hours later than they should have. And here he was with Ariel in his arms, hers wrapped around his neck. She never went to Scout like that unless she was really scared.

"What happened?"

Scout came over and deposited her on the bed beside me. Ariel cuddled in against me and settled down like she was ready for a nap or something. I raised an eyebrow at the still-silent Scout as he took a seat beside me, looking guilty as hell.

"Well, our little angel, here, decided to go for an adventure this morning."

Ariel stiffened against me, her little body going unnaturally still, which set off all of my inner mom alarms.

"What kind of adventure?"

"She heard me on the phone saying I was going to the clubhouse, so she decided to go visit her momma while I did my thing."

My mouth dropped open. Ariel went out alone? All the way to the cemetery? I glared at Scout and he mouthed at me that he'd tell me more later then nodded down to Ariel, who was still holding herself rigid against me.

"She's worried we're mad at her."

I easily filled in what he didn't say. She was worried we were going to send her away now. This poor girl had some serious abandonment issues.

"Oh, sweetheart, I'm not mad at you. The thought of you out walking around town on your own scares the hell out of me. I'm certainly glad you're okay. But next time you feel like going to visit your momma, you need to ask us to take you, okay? You're too little to be out on your own. We love you, Ariel, and we want you to be safe."

Her little head nodded against me as she snuggled in closer, moving a hand to rest over my belly, which her brother dutifully nudged. Tears stung my eyes at the connection they had already. I wrapped my arm around her so I could stroke her back with my hand as I turned my attention back to my man, who was going to be hearing about it later that he didn't tell me the moment he realized Ariel had gone missing. Guilt that I wasn't there to either stop it from happening, or deal with the outcome rose up and clogged my throat. I cleared it and pushed the thoughts aside. There'd be time later, when I was alone, to work through my feelings.

"So, you've had a busy morning, then?"

He stroked his hands through his hair with a groan.

"Phone started ringing at six. I got a whole lotta sh—stuff down the clubhouse to deal with."

He never told me club business unless I needed to know for my own safety. I knew that was how it worked so I didn't push for more information. Honestly, I didn't want to know most of the time. But none of that changed the fact I hated seeing him so stressed out.

"You sleeping okay?"

He looked up and held my gaze. "I sleep like shit without you beside me, babe. You know that."

As much as I didn't like that he wasn't getting enough rest, my heart warmed that he couldn't fully relax without me.

"Yeah, I don't sleep so well without you, either. I love you."

He stood and leaned over me. I tilted my face up and he took my mouth with his for a deep kiss.

"Love you so much. Can't wait to have you back home, where you belong."

"You and me both." He had no idea how much I truly hated being stuck in here, unable to do anything. "So, I gather if you got early morning phone calls you need to run off and deal with something?"

With a grimace he sat back down and scrubbed a hand over his face.

"Yeah, unfortunately I do. But it shouldn't take too long, then I'll be back."

Obviously, I wasn't the only one feeling guilt over what happened this morning. I knew Scout doubted himself as a father. He was an awesome dad to Ariel, but he couldn't see it in himself. Her running away from him this morning would have gutted him, and clearly, he didn't want to leave either one of us today. But he had responsibilities outside of me and Ariel that he needed to go deal with. I knew that going in with Scout, that there would be times he'd have to go deal with club business when we'd both prefer him stay with me. But we'd both feel better after he went and dealt with whatever shit it was that brought on the attack in my cafe.

I reached my hand out to grab his. "Scout, I understand you have responsibilities with the club, and that what happened in my cafe would have stirred up trouble. You need to go do what you have to so when our boy comes into this world, we're not looking over our shoulders, waiting for these bastards to come back for us."

He nodded slowly and his gaze settled on Ariel.

"We'll be fine, babe. Ariel and I will do some more handwriting practice, and maybe some drawing."

Her head popped up. "You'll read to me?"

I stroked my fingers down her cheek. "Of course, baby girl."

In the cult, Ariel hadn't had a chance to do any schooling at all. Thankfully she was still young, so wasn't too far behind, but we wanted her to fit in with the other kids when she started in September. So I spent some time with her every day, doing little things like learning how to write her name and numbers. I was trying to make it fun for her, and since she was so starved for affection, she'd loved every moment of it so far.

Scout stood and lifted the bag he'd brought with them onto the bed so we could reach it without any trouble.

"Here's all your things, Ariel. I'll leave you to it. I'll try to get back as soon as I can and we'll go shopping later for some flowers for your Momma, okay?"

Oh, that melted my heart in a second. My man was so beautiful. I knew he must be feeling so guilty, and I was too. We hadn't taken Ariel back to her mother's grave many times. Clearly, we needed to change that. No matter how difficult it was for us to be reminded of how badly we'd both failed Sarah in the past, Ariel's need to stay connected to her mother was more important.

Scout

By the time I walked through the front door of the clubhouse, I was spoiling for a fight. Or something. Anything to take the edge off. My woman, the other half of my fucking soul, was stuck in a hospital bed, and the girl I'd adopted and promised to take care of had run away from home. Away from me. Fuck, it felt like I'd failed Sarah all over again, along with Marie and Ariel.

Tiny was sitting with Mac at the bar when I came in so I headed over to them to get a status report from Tiny on our guest.

"Hey, prez, Ariel doing okay?"

"Yeah. She heard my side of our conversation and got it in her head I'd forgotten about her, so she took off. We found her at the cemetery, at Sarah's grave."

The big man winced. "Fuck. Poor kid."

"Pretty much. So, I need to get this shit dealt with so I can get back to her and Marie."

Bash was behind the bar and he set a drink in front of me that I tossed back in one gulp.

"Thanks, man. Okay, Mac, Tiny, let's get this shit done and over with."

With a rap of my knuckles on the bar, I turned and marched toward the back of the clubhouse where the hidden stairs were, confident Mac and Tiny were on my heels. The second I cracked the door I could hear Rumble hollering from his cell.

"Shit. You weren't kidding, were you?"

"Nope. He ain't stopped since he worked out his buddy died."

No wonder they'd been at the bar drinking. No one liked listening to a man suffering like this. Clearly, Rumble and Tank had been close. On days like this it sucked to be president. I knew what had to be done. Knew the decision I had to make. But I hated having to take a life. It was so fucking unnecessary. All these two clowns had to do was fucking come straight to me to ask for an audience. They didn't even need to come down here. Their fucking dipshit of a president should have picked up his damn phone and called me first. Not fucking declare war on us like this. Really, these two poor bastards were just following orders. But this was MC life. There were consequences for actions. Especially when you came after our women. They were innocent and should be left out of club business.

Rolling my neck, I climbed down the stairs behind Tiny, who had the key for the cells. I was just beginning to consider shoving my fingers in my ears when we got to the door and Tiny had the thing open. He moved back and I stepped past him, into the cell.

"Shut the fuck up already."

Rumble was looking worse for wear. The boys had given him some water over his stay down here, but that was it. And it looked like they'd taken a few shots at him too, if the bruising on his torso was any indication. His face was red and blotchy from his screaming and crying over his fallen brother.

"He's dead!"

"Yeah, well, he did take a baseball bat the head. Not sure what kinda women your club has, but our old ladies are nearly as tough as us men. As you and your buddy have seen, thinking our women are our weak link was a big, fucking mistake." I pointed to the body lying on the floor across the cell. "That, right there, was done by a woman. Call yourselves fucking enforcers. Neither of you were watching your backs, were you? Tell me,

Rumble, did you even notice our woman come up behind Tank before she landed her blow?"

There was fury behind the man's eyes. I knew rubbing in the fact they were taken down by a woman would work in getting him riled up. Dent the fucker's ego and pride some before we killed him. I might not like having to take a man's life, but if the fucker was stupid enough to come after my woman—risk her, my fucking unborn son along with two brothers' old ladies—well, he was going to go down hard.

"There was no rear door to the cafe, how the fuck were we supposed to know there's some secret fucking door back there that couldn't be seen from the outside."

I took a step closer. "There is no way. And anyone who's had any fucking training at all would have known that there's no way to know the interior layout from the outside and would have kept an eye on their six. But you wanna know the best part? You know who alerted our own little Harley Quinn to the fact she needed to come in swinging? A five-year-old girl. You can go to your fucking grave knowing you got taken down because a five-year-old girl stepped up. Didn't see her either, did you? My kid's good. She not only snuck out the back, but grabbed the baby who was there and took her too. You're a fucking disgrace."

He tried to pull from the chair, to stand and lunge at me.

"You fucking bastard. You said if I answered you, I'd walk outta here."

I shook my head. "No, I said there was more than one way to kill a man. Never said you'd live through this. You fucking took three of our women hostage, causing harm to all three of them, sent my old lady into early labor, risking my fucking son. You think we're just gonna fucking stand back and let you walk after that?"

He stilled and his eyes went hard. "My club will come for us. They will come and wreak havoc on every single Charon they can find."

I leaned in, getting my face right in front of his, but far enough away he couldn't head butt me. Not that he was smart enough to think of trying that.

"Not if we go after them first. Gonna end your whole fucking club for this stunt. The Ice Riders MC will be nothing but a memory and a lesson on why you don't fuck with the Charon MC by the end of the month. I promise you, we will end this war you started."

I pulled back as Mac took Rumble's head in his hands and twisted, snapping his neck.

"Enjoy hell, fucking bastard." I turned my attention to Mac. "Where'd his cut go?"

"Taz took it off to fix his shoulder. We stripped off Tank's after he died. We figured you'd want them. They're locked up in the safe, out of sight."

I nodded and glanced between the two dead men. "Guess we better get to disposing of these two fuckers."

We didn't kill people very often thankfully, but we did it often enough we had a system in place. It was fairly simple. And really, if you thought about it, it truly was way too easy to make a body disappear. A friend of the club, Ted, had a large ranch not far outside of town. He had a large manure piles that grew each day when the stalls were mucked. So we just added a little more organic material to the piles. We'd borrow his tractor, push the shit back, dig a shallow grave for the body, dump it and pull the manure back over it. Within two to three weeks there was nothing left. The first few times we tried it, we went back out there to check if it had worked, and it had, so thankfully we didn't have to check anymore. And ol' Ted knew if we'd shifted his manure into a new pile, he needed to leave it the fuck alone for a month, just to be sure.

Along with Tiny and Mac, I headed upstairs to get changed. Disposing of bodies got messy and damn smelly, so you didn't want to wear anything that you wanted to wear again when you did it. We'd all burn any of our clothes that got anything on them when we got back from dealing with the bodies. It simply wasn't worth the risk to keep them. Although, I doubted anyone was going to miss those two, at least, not once we'd dealt with their club. Which got me thinking—I hadn't heard anything about what happened to whatever transport they had brought down with them, assuming they didn't fly and rent something. I hoped they hadn't. That paper trail would take a little more effort to cover up.

When I got back downstairs, Tiny and Mac were both there, changed and ready to go.

"Did we locate their rides?"

"Yeah, looks like they rode down. The bikes were taken to the shop and the boys have already started stripping them down."

I nodded to Mac, relieved it had been handled. Having a well-functioning club to back you up was a beautiful thing.

"Excellent. Right, let's move out and get this shit done."

Chapter 8

Marie

The days following Ariel's little adventure were thankfully peaceful. Scout had come back that afternoon, and as promised, he'd taken Ariel out shopping for flowers before taking her back to visit Sarah's grave. Over the next few days he'd brought Ariel in as usual, but unlike the previous times, he now stayed with us. I'd asked him if he needed to go deal with club stuff that first day, and he'd told me it could all wait. That Ariel and I were more important. My man continued to melt my heart. I hated that we'd wasted so many years, that we could have had this decades ago. Although, maybe if we had gotten together in our twenties, we wouldn't have been ready for it. Life would have happened, and we might not have been together now. I mentally pushed the thoughts away. Everything happened when it was meant to and I needed to focus on what we had now, not what might have been.

That had me remembering yesterday with a smile. Zara had come in with Cleo for a visit, and they'd taken

Ariel down to the cafeteria to eat, and Scout had taken full advantage. He'd flipped that lock and was on me at lightning speed. I squirmed in the bed at the memory, wishing he was here now to relive it with me. Then, in a flash, all my arousal fled and I blew out a breath when a tightness set in across my lower belly. *Not again.*

A light knock on the door had me looking that way as I continued to clutch my belly. It was early morning, and the nurse was right on time for her rounds.

"Are you okay?"

"Something's happening."

I didn't know how to explain what was happening, but thankfully the nurse didn't seem to mind my vagueness.

"Let's get the doctor paged."

She came over and pressed the call button, telling the nurse who came rushing in a moment later to go find my doctor. Then she turned her full attention on me and her expression was so serious I was instantly scared something was wrong. It had been seven days since they'd stopped my labor. The doctor had said he wanted to try to hold off for at least a week to let the drugs work their magic. And I'd followed orders. Despite not wanting to be stuck here in hospital, I'd sucked it up, stayed in bed and barely moved all week. I'd done everything they'd told me, yet it seemed like I still managed to fail my boy.

"How about you give that man of yours a call? Get him in here."

Guilt and fear swirled in my mind and with tears pricking my eyes, I snatched up my mobile as she started doing tests, checking the baby's heartbeat and other stuff.

"Hey, beautiful lady, what's up?"

"I think I just had a contraction. The doctor isn't here yet—"

"I'm on my way."

"Please hurry."

"Be there before you know it, baby. Love you and you're going to be fine. So's our boy."

"Love you too, Charlie."

I hung up just as the doctor came rushing in.

"You have excellent timing, Marie. I was already on the floor for my morning rounds, so was close by. Right, let's see what's going on here, shall we?"

Before he even touched me, I felt a wet warmth between my legs.

"I think my water just broke!"

Panic quickly set in, speeding up my breathing. This was happening. My baby boy was coming and I wasn't ready. Scout wasn't here. I pressed a hand to my chest, trying to get more air in my lungs.

"Marie, look at me. It's going to be fine, but you need to take some deep breaths for me." I focused on the nurse and forced myself to concentrate on my breathing. "We need you calm so we can focus on bringing this baby of yours into the world."

I nodded but kept my gaze locked on her, refusing to even look at what the doctor or the other nurse were doing as I continued to focus on my breathing and remaining calm. For my son.

Scout

The second I hung up from Marie I was out of bed and reaching for my jeans. Stumbling as I rushed to dress, I made my way out into the hallway and down to Ariel's room. She was still sleeping so I let her be, continuing on my way to the kitchen where I sat to put my boots on. I called Mac, putting the phone between my shoulder and ear so I could do up my laces while it rang.

"What's wrong?"

Yeah, it was a bit early to be calling if everything was right in the world.

"Marie just called. She's in labor so I need to get to the hospital asap, but Ariel's still sleeping. Can you send Zara over to stay with her? Bring her in later for me?"

I'd sorted out with Mac that I'd drop Ariel off with him and Zara when Marie went into labor, but I really didn't want to wake her up if I didn't have to.

"Sure thing. I'll send her over now and I'll come over with Cleo in a bit. We'll bring Ariel in the minute you let us know we can."

"Thanks, brother."

Hanging up, I finished with my boots before jogging back up to my room where I'd left my wallet and keys. When I passed Ariel's room on my way back, I glanced inside and saw she was rubbing her eyes. Not wanting a repeat of earlier in the week, I went in and kneeled beside her bed.

"Hey, angel, I need to tell you something." I waited for her to roll over and face me. "Mommy just called, and it looks like your brother is gonna be born soon. I have to go to the hospital to help her, but unfortunately you can't go with me. So Zara is going to come over and look after you until the doctor tells me you're allowed to come visit. Okay?"

I was twisting the truth a little, but the last thing Ariel needed to see was childbirth in all its gory detail. I also knew if I didn't explain it right, she'd get it in her head that I was abandoning her again. I didn't want that for her.

"Okay, Papa."

"That's my girl. Love you, Ariel, and I promise, I'll call Zara to bring you in the moment it's possible."

I gave her a kiss on her temple then I was up and out of her room, rushing to the front door where Zara was now knocking. I grabbed my helmet and opened the door.

"Hey, Zara, thanks for this. Ariel's just waking up now. I've told her what's happening so hopefully she'll stay calm for you." *And not run away again.*

"I'm sure we'll be just fine. You go help Marie bring your baby into the world safely and we'll see you later."

I gave her a quick hug and she kissed my cheek before, with a nod, I left her to go to Ariel as I headed to my bike. I got my helmet on and the beast started in record time, despite the fact my hands were trembling. The ride over to the hospital was a blur, and before I knew it, I was racing through the halls to Marie's room.

"Mr. Dalton!"

I barely heard the nurse as I skidded into Marie's room. My heart nearly stopped when I took in the empty space. Throwing out an arm, I braced myself against the door frame. She had to be all right.

"Mr. Dalton!"

I turned toward the woman calling out to me.

"Where is she? What's happened?"

"The baby was showing signs of distress so the doctor has her in an operating room, prepping her for an emergency c-section. If you'll follow me, I'll take you to her. We should be able to get you there in time for the birth."

With a nod, I followed her down the hall. I wanted to run, to sprint, to get to my woman's side and make sure I was there in time. But since I didn't know where the fuck she was, I was forced to walk beside the nurse. At least the woman was walking quickly.

A mix of excitement, fear and nerves churned inside me as I followed her directions to wash up and then donned the smock thing she handed me. When she passed me what looked like two shower caps, I raised an eyebrow at her.

"The operating room is a sterile environment. For your baby's protection you'll need to cover your beard and your hair. This one is designed to go over your beard. I know it's not exactly the height of fashion, but it's for Marie and the baby's safety."

That's all I needed to know. I'd do anything to keep them safe, even look like a fool. As quickly as possible I put them both on, then, finally, she led me into the operating room. Marie was set up on the operating table, a blue drape hanging from a stand above her, down to her boobs, blocking her view of what they were going to do to her belly. Her face was pale and her eyes wide. My heart clenched at how scared my poor woman looked, lying there helpless.

The second I came in, she looked to me and bit her lip as she struggled to get her hand out from under the covers. I lunged forward and took her hand in mine before she could bump something she probably shouldn't. I stroked my other palm over her face, wiping her tears away while being careful to not mess with the oxygen tube fitted under her nose.

"Hey, darlin'."

I stalled out after that. The beard cover covered my mouth and muffled my words some. On top of that, I had no fucking clue what to say to take away the fear that shone in her eyes. Despite wanting to assure her everything was going to be fine, I didn't know if it would be and I refused to lie to her and give her empty promises. Thankfully the doctor saved me from my dilemma.

"Excellent. Perfect timing! We've just finished getting the epidural sorted and are ready to start. Take a seat and let's bring this boy into the world. Tell me, have you chosen a name yet?"

The anesthetist rolled a stool closer to me and I sat down, before stroking Marie's face again.

"Joey. We're naming him Joey Ronald Dalton."

Even though she couldn't see it, I grinned. When we'd discussed names, Marie had wanted our boy to have her foster father's name as his middle one. I agreed, Ronald had raised Marie, despite her not being his biological daughter. And he'd gone above and beyond to keep her safe when she'd fucked up with the Iron Hammers, even though she'd aged out of the system and he didn't have to. He sadly wasn't with us anymore, but he deserved this honor Marie wanted to give him. Joey had been a name she'd always loved, and I couldn't come up with anything better so Joey it is. My woman was way too sweet for the likes of me. I was still quite certain I didn't deserve her, but fuck it all, she was mine and I was keeping her forever.

"Great name. Let's meet, him shall we?"

As the doctor and nurses went to work behind the drape, I stayed focused on Marie, watching every twitch and wince she made as the staff did their thing. I hated I couldn't take this from her, go through it myself in her place. But it wasn't possible, so I did what I could. I sat there, holding her hand, letting her crush my fingers while I stroked her face and held her gaze with mine.

I have no idea how long it took, but I'll never forget the moment the doctor told her she'd feel some pressure, then the sweetest sound I'd ever heard reached my ears. My son's cry.

Marie started sobbing and I did nothing to stop the flow of my own tears.

"Is he okay?"

"He looks good."

The nurse briefly held him up over the top of the drape for us and I'd never seen anything so beautiful in all my life. Covered in muck with his face scrunched up in displeasure, he was still utterly perfect.

"Babe, you did good. He's so beautiful."

Pulling the material over my mouth down, I bent to kiss her, not caring that my tears were dropping onto her face. I whispered my love for her before I rose up and let the cover flick back up over my mouth. Then the nurse wheeled the table thing they had Joey on next to us and we watched as they wiped him down and did their tests and shit.

My heart expanded more with every second I watched my boy. I had a son. Marie, my beautiful, perfect wife, had gifted me with the ultimate, most precious gift. Ariel was my daughter, I loved her as if she were my own, but I hadn't been there when she came into the world. This feeling right now, being here from the very beginning of

Joey's life, it was on a whole new level and had me feeling things I'd never felt before and had no idea how to articulate.

Once they were done, they wrapped his wee little body up in a blanket and brought him over to us. In less than a heartbeat, my palms were out. I wanted to hold my boy. The nurse lifted up the tiny bundle of baby and placed him in my hands.

"He's so light. And tiny."

"Hey, baby boy, look at you."

Marie reached up and stroked a finger down his nose, then I shifted his little body up so she could give him a kiss on the cheek.

"See you again soon, baby boy. Mommy loves you."

Before I was ready, the nurse took him from me and placed him in a bassinet. The doctor had explained earlier that he'd need to go down to NICU after the birth. I was completely torn on what to do. Did I stay with Marie or follow our son? I wanted to split myself in two so I could do both.

"Go, Charlie. Stay with Joey. I'm gonna be fine. Doc will sew me up, then I'll go chill in recovery for bit. I know if I could, I'd be following Joey."

Her voice broke at the end. My poor woman, she wanted so bad to not be separated from our son but forces outside our control wouldn't allow it.

"I'll always take care of you both, Marie. I wish I could be in both places at the same time."

She reached up and pulled the cloth away from my mouth.

"But you can't, so kiss me and go take care of our boy. He needs his papa."

"I love you, Marie."

I did what I was told, kissing her hard and fast before heading for the door, following the nurse pushing my son's bassinette.

Chapter 9

Ariel

"You ready to meet your little brother?"

Butterflies were going crazy in my tummy as I jumped up and down.

"Oh, yes, Papa. Where is he? Where's Mommy?"

After Papa had called Mac to let him know I was allowed to go in, he, Zara and baby Cleo had piled into their car with me and came straight to the hospital so I could meet my brother. I stopped jumping and squeezed harder on Zara's hand as I looked around the empty hallway. Where were they? I noticed Papa when he crouched down and took my other hand in his.

"Well, sweet angel, when babies come early like your brother did, they need to come down here to what is called the NICU. It's a special part of the hospital where they look after babies who come early or are sick. Only babies are allowed to stay down here, so Mommy is back in her room, waiting for us to come tell her everything about him."

I gave him a small nod and let go of Zara to move toward Papa, who picked me up. I loved how big and strong he was and I really liked it when he held me like this. Like his big, strong arms would keep me safe. I hadn't been sure I could trust him to start with but he'd shown me since I came to live with him and Mommy that I could. I'd especially liked this past week with him. He'd spent a lot of time with me and Mommy in her hospital room. He'd read stories and twice after we left Mommy, he took me to go buy pretty sunflowers for Momma, and we went and put them on her grave.

As the glass doors whooshed open and Papa walked in, I looked over his shoulder and smiled when I saw that Mac, who was still holding baby Cleo, and Zara, were following us.

My tummy twisted up in knots and I tightened my grip on Papa as he brought me up to a plastic cage with a baby inside. I gasped at all the wires on the little body. Who would be so cruel?

"Why is he stuck in there? And the wires? Why is he being hurt? We need to get him out, Papa. He's hurting!"

I wriggled, trying to get down. If he wouldn't help my brother, I would.

"Shh, sweetheart. He's just fine where he is. Calm down and I'll explain why." Papa stopped talking until I stopped trying to break free of his hold. "Look at his face. He's peacefully sleeping. He's showing no sign of being in any pain."

I forced my gaze to focus on his face and saw that Papa was right. He sure didn't look like he was in pain. Papa moved right up close to him, close enough I could press my palm on the glass and really see him.

"When babies come early, sometimes parts of their body aren't fully formed yet. We were very lucky. Your brother just needs a little time in the incubator to help his lungs get enough oxygen. All the wires are attached to the little stickers, not poking into his skin. They're small sensors to pick up his heart rate and other things so the doctors and nurses can make sure that he's doing okay."

A nurse came over to us and I tensed when I saw she held one of the stickers.

"Here's what your brother has on him. You can have this one." I took the little sticky square from her hand and frowned down at it. "Why don't you put it on the back of your hand? See what it feels like, so you can be sure we didn't do anything to hurt your baby brother."

Papa thanked the nurse while I did as she said, sticking the small patch on the back of my hand. It really did feel like a sticker. And nothing jabbed at me, even when I twisted my hand around. That made me smile up at Papa.

"You okay now, angel? You know I'd never let anything hurt either you or your brother, don't you?"

"I know, Papa. I just got scared when I first saw him. What's his name?"

Mommy wouldn't tell me before he was born, saying I couldn't keep it a secret. I was very good at keeping secrets. Mommy and Papa both tried to tell me it would be more fun this way, but I wasn't so sure.

"Joey Ronald Dalton."

I nodded as I said the name inside my head a few times. Joey. My baby brother.

"He's so pretty, Papa. When can I hold him?"

"Ah, not real sure, Ariel. Maybe in a few days' time, once he's a little stronger. I promise, outside of me and Mommy, you'll be the first to get a cuddle. Sound good?"

"Uh huh."

I looked down at Joey, leaning in so I could press a kiss to the glass. He was so tiny. He was going to need me to help keep him safe. I vowed that I'd never let anyone hurt him. I might only be five years old, and had Momma, who'd done her best to shield me, but I'd seen things. Felt things. Things I would never, ever let Joey see or feel.

"Can we go see Mommy now?"

With a chuckle, Papa shifted me in his grip so he could press his palm on the glass over Joey. After a few moments, he turned and we headed toward the exit.

"He's a good looking boy, prez."

I grinned as Mac spoke with Papa. Joey was perfect.

"He sure is. Takes after his mother."

I hugged Papa tighter. I thought he was perfect, too. Zara laughed and nudged Papa with her elbow. "You're not so bad, yourself, Scout. I love the name, very sweet.

And he looks good, bigger than I was expecting, considering he's early."

Papa chuckled. "Yeah, that he gets from me. Big and in a hurry to get where he's going."

"I took a few photos with my phone to show Marie."

"Thanks, brother. You're a life saver."

I stopped listening as the adults continued to speak. Instead, I started playing with the edges on the patches on Papa's vest as we moved through the hallways and thought about all the things I was going to do with my little brother when he was big enough to play with.

Marie

Taking a deep breath, I swiped the tears from my face and tried to control myself. I'd been moved from recovery back to my hospital room, but that meant I was all alone. Scout was down with Joey, Ariel was no doubt down there too, by now. But I was here. Stuck in a bed, unable to even get up and take myself to the toilet, let alone go care for either of my kids. I slapped my palm over my mouth when a sob broke free.

None of this was how I'd imagined it would be. I was supposed to carry Joey to term. Then when I went into labor, I'd be screaming for drugs while clutching Scout's hand. Followed by pure joy when I got to hold my son, to snuggle his little body in against me as Scout looked on proudly.

More tears flowed, and I squeezed my eyes closed against them. I'd failed. I'd failed my son and my husband. Fuck, I'd failed Sarah, too. How had I let her vanish like she had? I should have known she'd get into trouble out in the world on her own. But I'd been selfish, I hadn't wanted to leave Scout. Now I had her little girl to raise and I was already failing her. Ariel had needed me and I wasn't there. She'd run away, to the cemetery. To the grave of her mother, who even in death was doing a better job of being there for Ariel than I was.

"Oh, sweetheart."

Instantly I stilled, my runaway thoughts cut short as my gaze flew to the doorway where Donna stood. She came in, closing the door, before she made her way over to me. When she sat beside me on the mattress and leaned over with her arms out, I leaned forward and wrapped mine around her neck, letting my sobs out unchecked.

"Let it all out, sugar. Nothing good will come from bottling it all up."

I took her advice, I stopped trying to pull it back and just let it all out, soaking the shoulder of her top as my thoughts continued to twist and turn, tormenting me with all my shortcomings. Finally, my tears slowed, and with a hiccup, I pulled back from Donna, releasing her and laying back against the mattress, feeling drained but lighter for the release.

"Let me guess—you're feeling like you've failed because things didn't go to plan? I'll let you in on a secret, Marie. Very few of us get the dream. The ideal life we plan for when we're young girls, day-dreaming with our bestie. The trick is to roll with it. To let that dream change and know it's fine to veer off the path and find a new road."

As much as I'd seen and chatted with Donna at countless Charon family barbecues, I didn't really know her. She was Keys' old lady and their daughter, Emma, had been killed year before last when a heap of shit went down with Zara getting kidnapped. Naturally it was all club business so I didn't know what happened, other than the fact that Emma had been killed somehow in the mix.

"We've never really sat down and chatted, have we? Strange, since it looks like we have a lot in common. Did you know Keys wasn't Emma's biological father?"

I shook my head. I'd had no clue. Never once over all these years did I think Keys wasn't that girl's father in every sense of the word.

She scoffed a short laugh. "Yeah, my plan didn't turn out either. Like you, I grew up down in Galveston. I grew up rough. On the wrong side of the tracks. We never had any money so I did whatever I could to get a foot up. God, I wanted out of that life so bad. Bad enough that when a guy from down the street took a shine to me, told me he was rising up through the ranks of the Iron Hammers, I saw a way out. Damn, the shit I fell for back then. He spun some good ones, and I lapped every one of them up. For a while it was good. He was affectionate and protective. And true to his word, he was, indeed, rising up within the club. The day I found out I was pregnant, I was so excited. Figured he'd surely propose to me when he found out. I'd never been inside the clubhouse before that morning. He'd told me it wasn't the place for me, that I was too innocent and pretty for the place." She huffed out a breath. "More like he didn't want to change his ways for me. I walked in to find him balls deep in some random woman. It was ugly. I yelled at him, he yelled back, I slapped him and he hit me in return. I never did tell him about Emma. Just packed up and hitched a ride out of town. I didn't want to ever see him again."

"How'd you end up here? Meeting Keys?"

Her expression softened with a smile. "I'd heard my ex say often enough how much he hated the Charons that I'd figured Bridgewater was a safe place to go to get away from him. The Charons are good men. I was living on the streets, sleeping down in the park, when Keys found me. One of the men had noticed me down there doing it rough and they'd reported it back to the club. Keys was a prospect back then and they'd sent him out to pick me up and bring me in to meet with the president. I'd been so scared. Hadn't wanted to get anywhere near another MC. Keys was sweet. He'd left his bike there at the park, pocketed the keys and walked with me down to the motel where he paid for a room for me to stay in for the week."

She leaned over and grabbed a tissue to wipe her own face.

"It certainly wasn't my original plan, but I ended up with Keys so it worked out all right. By the time Emma arrived, Keys had moved me from the motel into his place. He was there when she was born. Of course, it would have been so much better if her biological father had stayed out of her life. But no, that bastard came back and took her from me."

Compared to her, I had nothing to whine about and suddenly felt about an inch tall for even complaining.

"I'm so sorry, Donna. You must think I'm so foolish for carrying on like I am. It's just, hell, I feel like I'm failing them all. Scout, Ariel, Joey, Sarah. I couldn't even hold on to the pregnancy to term! And now I'm up here on my own while they're all down in the NICU."

With a gentle smile, Donna gave my hand a pat. "Oh, honey. I don't think anything of the sort. We all have our trials—they're different, but no less painful. I came up here before Scout and Ariel made their way up because I had an inkling that you might be struggling. It's only natural. And you didn't fail anyone, Marie. Sarah made her choices, ones I'm sure she regretted but they're done and in the past. None of us had any control over those bastards coming into your cafe with guns out ready to cause trouble. You did good. All of you did. No one stirred them up to the point they started shooting and you all got out of there alive. You held on long enough for the drugs to do their thing and Joey looks really good, and he's big for a preemie. I went and had a peek in on him on my way up and had a quick word with your doctor. He's confident Joey's going to be just fine."

She was making it all sound so simple but it wasn't. Nothing about this was.

"Ariel ran away. She needed me and I wasn't there."

That got me another gentle smile. "Life happens, honey. Sometimes we can't be where we want to be. You were laid up here, unable to do much of anything. Scout had it under control. Granted, it took him a bit to get there, but he did. And thankfully Keys is a paranoid man who tags anything he can on the kids of the club. Well, the women and kids. I suspect he does it to his brothers too, but just doesn't tell any of them. I love that man, but I swear, he's got some serious issues about not being able to locate those he cares for." She shook her head.

"You only had Emma, right?"

I'd always been curious why they only had the one child. They were both such caring people, I could easily see them raising a whole heap of kids. She gave me a sad smile.

"Keys got really ill as a child. He never would tell me what exactly he had, but it ended up making him infertile. Guess that's why he always considered the fact I was already pregnant when he fell for me was a blessing." She chuckled. "Of course, he had no idea I was pregnant to begin with. I'd been petrified they'd send me back to the Hammers if they knew I carried one of theirs inside me. So I didn't say anything about being pregnant until after I started to show. When I did finally confide to Keys who the father was, I swore him to secrecy. I'm pretty sure he only ever told the previous president about her true paternity. Well, until Sledge opened his big ol' mouth after Zara's rescue and told everyone."

Holy shit! I tried not to let my mouth gape open in shock.

"Sledge? As in the former president of the Hammers? He was Emma's dad?"

She winced. "Yeah, we all make dumb decisions when we're young. If we're lucky, we get to live long enough to learn from them."

Before we could say anything more, the door opened and Ariel came bounding in.

"Mommy, Mommy, Mommy! He's soooo perfect!!! I love him so much!"

Hiding behind Donna for a moment, I wiped my face free of the last of my tears.

"Is that right, sweet angel?"

"Uh huh."

Donna moved to stand as Scout strolled in the room, Mac and Zara following with Cleo. Scout was wearing the broad grin of a man proud of himself. I couldn't help but return his smile. Donna was right. I knew she was. But it was going to take me a little bit to get my brain and emotions on board with the new plan. Thankfully I had a brilliant, strong man to support me while I did. I turned to face Ariel, who was still dancing around the room, clearly too riled up to sit still and give me the cuddle she normally did when she first came in. My eyes teared up again for a different reason as I watched her. I'd not seen her this alive since we first got her. This was what I wanted for her. This pure joy and carefree happiness all children should experience.

"Hey, babe. You okay?"

I waved off his concern. "Yeah, just having an emotional moment with Donna."

Scout leaned down and I tilted my face up to accept his kiss, instantly feeling better as his scent washed over me.

"Our boy's doing good. And he has his big sister firmly wrapped around his little finger already."

"I see that. Take a photo of her for me?"

Mac stepped up, pulling his phone out to snap a few shots while Ariel was still lost in her own world.

"I took some of her and Scout with Joey, too." He moved forward to hand me his phone to look through his photos. "Congratulations, Marie. He's a gorgeous boy."

"Thanks, Mac."

I scrolled through the photos, trying to not start crying all over again. The three of them were so sweet together.

"Enough already! Let me through." Zara all but shoved Scout off the side of the bed and took his place to give me a tight hug. "He's soo beautiful, Marie. Congratulations!"

With a smile, I locked my gaze with Scout's over Zara's shoulder. Life was pretty damn good. I had my dream man, a daughter and now a son. I just needed to

get the hell out of this damn hospital bed so I could go
enjoy it.

Chapter 10

Scout

My boy was just three days old when my phone rang and destroyed the little bubble of peace I'd been happily living in. I knew it was going to happen, but this past week had been nice. Just me, my girls and Joey. Even though Marie and Joey were still in hospital, it was still good. Especially now that Marie was able to get up and move around some, she could come down to the NICU and hold Joey. That seemed to help bring her out of her funk. She tried to hide it, but I knew she was struggling.

I would never forget the first time the nurses had me strip my shirt off so I could hold my son skin on skin. They told me it was good for Joey to have the contact. I didn't doubt it, considering it did wonders for me too. Just like I knew Marie loved holding him against her chest. She'd get the sweetest smile and her eyes would glaze over with tears every time. I'd never tire of watching them together.

But reality was here and I stepped out of the NICU to take the call that I knew was going to force me away.

"Hey, prez. I hate to interrupt your family time, but have you reached Parrish yet?"

"I've tried twice now, but it went to voicemail both times. I'll come down to the clubhouse now and try again."

"Did you want one of us to put the call through so you can stay there?"

"Nah, it should be me who calls him. And if he doesn't answer again, we'll work something else out. We need to get moving on dealing with this shit."

Jack Parrish was a good man, fucking nuts, but under that crazy, he was solid. He was the president of the Satan's Knights MC, and this issue with the Ice Riders was fucking serious, so the call needed to come from me as president. Rubbing my face, I returned to the NICU as I slipped my phone away. Before I could even say a word, Marie spoke up.

"You need to go in, right? It's okay, Scout. I understand and you've not dealt with the club for over a week now. They need you, and I need you to go deal with whatever caused those men to come into my cafe before Joey gets out of here."

My woman was one in a million. For real.

Fortunately, there was only one other baby in the NICU so there wasn't a heap of staff and other people hanging around to overhear us. Moving up close to Marie, I dropped down to my knees in front of her and gently stroked my fingers down Joey's head and back. His skin was so damn soft. His little face screwed up for a moment before he settled back to sleep on his mommy's chest.

"He's so beautiful, just like his mom."

She cupped my face in the hand not holding our son and tilted it up until my gaze caught hers.

"I love you, Charlie. And I know you'd rather stay here with us, but you have more than just us relying on you. I know who I married. Go and make sure those bastards can't ever hurt any of our family again."

My woman was so fucking gorgeous, it made my eyes water. Standing up, I leaned down and took her mouth with mine, wrapping a hand around the back of her neck to hold her still for me while I kissed her deeply. Arousal ripped through me, leaving my cock throbbing for her. With a groan, I tore my lips from hers, resting my forehead against hers as I glanced down at our sleeping boy. I needed to go do this. For Marie, for Joey and Ariel. For all my Charon family.

I stood up before I spoke again.

"Okay, I'm going. I'll be back as soon as I can."

"Bring Ariel with you?"

Ariel was spending the day with Rose, Bulldog's wife.

I gave her a nod. "Yeah, I'll make sure I'm in time to bring her in. You ready to come home?"

I knew she was torn about being discharged before Joey was. I felt the same damn way every time I had to leave the hospital without either of them. She wanted to stay with Joey, but she wanted to come home with me and Ariel at the same time.

"I'm going to miss him. And I hate that he can't come home with us."

"Yet. He's strong and doing well. It won't be long before he's ready to come home with us."

My heart ached when a tear slipped from her eye. I wiped it from her cheek before lowering to give her one last kiss, all the while wishing like hell I could give her what we both wanted—Joey well enough that he could come home.

"I know this isn't how we planned for things to go, but it's what we've been dealt. And I swear to you, Marie, it'll all work out. We'll have our boy home with us before you know it."

My phone ringing again had me growling at the thing.

"Okay, I really gotta go."

I gave Joey a light kiss to the top of his head, before giving Marie a final peck to her lips, then I turned and left them. It gutted me to walk away and I knew I was leaving my fucking heart behind with them. I wished I could stay there with them, but shit needed to be done. For them. To keep them safe and to seek vengeance and justice against those who'd forced my son to be born early and robbed my old lady of her dream of being able to bring him into the world naturally, and take him home with us, healthy, a few days later.

By the time I made it to my office, Arrow, Mac and Tiny had joined me.

"How're Marie and Joey doing?"

Typically, Arrow got straight to the point.

"Good. Marie's coming home later today. Joey's doing well, but the doctor wants him in the incubator for a while longer yet. It's killing Marie to not be able to bring him home."

Arrow leveled his all too seeing gaze on me. "She's not the only one it's hurting."

I sighed and scrubbed my palms over my face. "It's a fucking mess, brother. My old lady's miserable and trying to hide it from me. Ariel freaked the fuck out that her brother is living in a plastic box. Poor kid thought he was being hurt with all the wires. And Joey's still in that damn thing. So yeah, I'm hurting. But there ain't a fucking thing I can do about any of that, so I'm gonna work on what I can do—making those fucking assholes pay for coming after what's mine."

I didn't want to talk about it. Once Arrow got going, he could talk a man's ear off. I slid my phone out and cursed when I saw the missed call from earlier was from Parrish. At least that hopefully meant he was around to answer my call this time. I pulled up his contact details and hit send. Holding the phone to my ear, I mentally begged the man to fucking pick up. I really didn't want to send my men up there with nowhere for them to land.

"Parrish."

Relief coursed through me at the growled word and I leaned back in my seat.

"Hey, Parrish. Scout from the Charon MC down in Texas. How's things?"

"They're completely fucked."

"Sorry to hear that."

Nerves had me leaning forward to rest my elbows on my desk. I held Arrow's gaze. I wasn't sure what the hell we were gonna do if Parrish's plate was already full and he couldn't help us at all.

"It is what it is. Seems like you've been doing your damnedest to get in touch with me. While I appreciate the gesture, I gotta wonder why."

Stroking my beard for a moment I tried to figure out how to best ask for his help, without giving away too much over an open phone line, but saying enough to get him on board.

"Ten days ago my old lady's cafe was attacked. She and two other of the club's women were working when two enforcers from a club up in Boston came storming in. Two of our fucking kids were in there too, not that the fuckers cared. They came in with guns out, ready to start a fucking war."

Parrish growled but didn't say anything, so I continued.

"Our kids are good, snuck out the back and got to safety. The women are fine now. Zara got a few cuts and bruises, Mercedes went into shock. My woman was thirty-three weeks pregnant and ended up going into early labor. They stopped it but it didn't hold and our son was born last Wednesday. He's doing okay, still in the hospital, but he's looking good."

"Sorry to hear that, brother, but I gotta be straight with you. I don't get why you're calling me with this. I'm not exactly your neighbor."

"Ever heard of the Ice Riders MC? They got a charter up in Boston."

"Name rings a bell. Never had any dealings with them, though. You telling me they're the ones who came after your women?"

"Yeah, they did. We've taken care of the two that came down here, but we want to end this shit permanently, if you get my drift."

"I hear you loud and clear, Scout. Thing is, I'm not sure what I can do to help. I'm up to my ears in my own shit. My old lady was in a car wreck that left her in a coma. She woke up a few days ago with traumatic amnesia. I'm shuffling between the hospital and taking care of our son."

I winced and shook my head. Fuck, what a mess.

"Fuck, I'm sorry to hear that, Parrish. I hope she makes a full recovery, and quickly too. Fuck. You thinking accident or set up?"

He was quiet for a moment, not responding at all, which was all the response I needed. He either knew or at least suspected it wasn't an accident.

"Look, here's where I'm at. I can't leave Marie and my boy at the moment, so I wanna send up four of my men. At this point, all I'm asking for is you give them a place to land when they get in. Arrow will fill you in on the rest of what's going on once they get there and maybe we can find a way to help each other out of all this shit, yeah?"

"Yeah, sounds good. Give me names. Who you sending me?"

"Mac and Tiny, it was their women in the cafe. Arrow, my club treasurer, and a prospect, Bash. I'll sort out their plane tickets now and I'll let you know when they're due to land."

"Have them fly into Newark and I'll have a man pick 'em up. They'll stay with me, at my place, until my wife is released. If they're still here when that happens, I'll figure out arrangements for them."

I nodded, even though he couldn't see me. "Sounds good. Appreciate it, Parrish."

"I got you, brother."

We ended the call and I turned to Arrow.

"Book the tickets for you four, as soon as you can. Parrish said to fly in to Newark and he'll send someone to pick you up. Let me know what time and I'll pass it on to him. Mac, Tiny? You two best go tell your women you'll be out of town for a while. No fucking clue how long this shit will take to handle. I'll go find Bash and tell him the good news. Oh, and Mac? I want you to take the keys out of the NY Mob and Ice Rider ledgers with you. I'll get Silk to sign forms giving you her authority for the boxes. Just in case."

With the way life was going lately, it was better he have those keys and be able to go to the safety deposit boxes John left for Silk. It would give him the physical copies of the ledgers, cash and maybe an extra weapon or two. Things they'll no doubt need, because the Ice Riders might have started this fucking war, but we would be ending it.

Marie

It felt like I was missing a limb or something. Sure, I was glad to be home and out of hospital but without Joey here too, it didn't feel right. Ariel was clearly ecstatic to have me back home. She'd danced her way through her night-time routine and had nearly glowed with happiness when I'd read her two bedtime stories. I suspect Scout hadn't caught onto the fact our little girl loved getting a bonus story each night. I knew he'd tried hard to keep up with everything I normally did with Ariel, but little things like the second story each night he hadn't known about without me around, and Ariel had been too shy to ask him for.

But now she was tucked in for the night and I found myself standing outside Joey's room, staring at the crib and changing table. The rocking chair Scout had bought and put together for me. The bassinet that we'd move to our room for the first month or so, once he come home. I stepped inside the room and went over to the table, raising my hand to run my fingers over the stack of tiny diapers and the super soft towel with the little blue bunnies on it that Ariel had picked out for her brother.

"Babe? What are you doing in here?"

Scout's strong arms snaked around my middle as he'd spoken, and with a sigh I leaned back against him.

"I miss him."

He turned me in his arms then pressed a kiss to my temple, his beard tickling my face and making me smile a little as I reached up to run my fingers through the soft hair to smooth it down.

"Me, too, love. It was worse when you weren't here, either. The place just felt empty. And it won't feel complete until we bring Joey home where he's meant to be." He tightened his arms around me. "But don't worry, it won't be long. The doctor and all the nurses are confident he's going to be discharged soon."

I nodded as I snuggled in against him, tangling my fingers in his shirt as I inhaled the scent that was Scout. From what the doctor had last told us, Joey was mostly being kept in as a precaution at this stage. The rule of thumb was that preemie babies stayed in hospital until their due date, but I was hoping they'd ease up on that particular rule and let us bring him home early. Of course, I wasn't going to push the issue. If Joey needed another week or two in the incubator to make sure his lungs were fully developed and functioning correctly, then that's what he'd get. As much as I wanted him home, I refused to risk his long-term health for it.

"C'mon, love. Let's go to bed. We both could use a good night's sleep, I'm sure."

With a nod, I let him guide me out of Joey's room and up the hallway to ours. I stalled out again when I gripped the bottom of my shirt to lift over my head. Scout hadn't seen my scar yet, and my tummy was still swollen. I watched as he stripped off his shirt, revealing all his glorious muscles that were as toned now as they'd always been. Swallowing my nerves, I tightened my grip on the material as Scout twisted to toss his shirt into the hamper. As he flicked open his belt and fly, he turned and his gaze ran over me before with a frown, he strode over toward me.

"Marie? What's wrong, love? Are you in pain? Can I get you something?"

Tears pricked my eyes at how sweet this man always was with me. On one level, I knew how stupid it was to even question how he felt about me. But I couldn't help it. My own view on my body had changed, so why wouldn't his too?

"I'm different."

His frown deepened. "I'm not sure I get what you mean."

"They *cut* Joey out of me."

His gaze lowered to where I had my hands splayed over my shirt, pressing the material against the scar. After a moment of silence, his expression softened and he wrapped his fingers around mine, peeling them away. Staying silent, he lifted my shirt up and off before he dropped to his knees. My body stiffened and my breath caught at him being so close to the ugly, healing wound. He slowly lowered my pants, leaving my underwear with the thick pad in it behind. He lifted each foot and stripped them away, leaving me feeling completely exposed in just my nursing bra and panties. It wasn't just my body on display in that moment, but my heart and soul too.

Goose bumps rose on my skin when he ran his large, rough palms up my legs. Wrapping them around my hips, he held me in place as he looked up, locking his gaze with mine.

"Marie, babe, I love every single inch of you. Inside and out. There is *nothing*, and I mean nothing at all that could change how I feel about you. Least of all a scar you earned by bringing our boy safely into this world."

He leaned forward and pressed the lightest of kisses to the edge of the scar and my tears broke free as a sob wracked my body. He was too much, too perfect, and I wasn't.

"Ah, love. It's okay. Everything's gonna be just fine."

He stood and wrapped one arm behind my knees and the other around my back, lifting me up against him. Rolling into his body, I wrapped my arms around his neck and buried my face in against his soft beard. I clung to him as he moved across the room. When my back was against our bed, he peeled my hands from around his neck and stood straight.

"Give me a minute to strip off, love."

Snuffling as I tried to stop crying, I watched him peel his jeans down, then tug off his socks. The full frontal view I got when he came back to bed was good enough it had me sighing, which made him smirk and take his thick erection in his hand.

"You want this, babe? 'Cause I fucking want you more than I want to breathe, but we gotta wait. I won't risk hurting you, love. Doc says six weeks. It's gonna be a long, fucking six weeks, but we'll do it."

He was crazy, but I appreciated his lightening the mood. With a smile, I lifted my arms up, beckoning him to me.

"We can still cuddle, and you can still kiss me whenever you want."

Pressing a knee to the edge of the bed, he dropped his weight onto his hands then crawled over until I was caged beneath him. With a wide grin, I wound my arms around his neck and twirled my fingers in the short hair above his neck. His eyes sparkled as he smiled down at me.

"Is that right? Whenever I like, huh? What about *wherever* I like?"

When I nodded, he lowered down and kissed across my collarbone before working his way up my neck, to my mouth. The feel of his hot, smooth skin against mine had my blood singing in my veins. When his lips finally found mine, I groaned as I opened my mouth and let him in.

Scout sure was an expert at kissing. Every time was perfect. Whether it was hard and fast because we didn't have much time, or a long, drawn-out seduction, like he was doing now, it didn't matter. Either way melted my heart and revved up my body.

It truly was going to be a long six weeks.

Chapter 11

Marie

I hated watching Scout struggle. He'd dropped me at the hospital before he headed out to take Mac, Arrow, Tiny and Bash to the airport. I knew he wanted to be going with them, and I loved him all the more for the fact he was choosing to stay home with the kids and me.

After all, he was the president of the Charons, so I wouldn't have been surprised if he had decided to go with them in the end. He took his role with the club seriously, making sure he kept all his Charon family as safe as he could at all times, just like he was deadly serious about keeping us protected. So if he had decided he needed to go up there to take out this threat personally, I would have understood. But luckily for me, he put his place as my husband and the kids' father above all else this time.

Even though I would have understood him going, I was damn relieved he was staying close to home. I hoped the four men who were going all returned safely, but it was always a risk they wouldn't. Zara was one of my closest friends, as was Mercedes, and both their men were heading up to New York. Add to that, the doctor hadn't cleared me to go back to work, so they were running my cafe on their own. I was worried about overworking the pair of them.

Scout had told me how the club had gone in and cleaned up the mess that was left after the attack, making sure everything was back to how it should be, which I was grateful for. Zara and Mercedes had enough to do without having to clean up blood and garbage off the floor from the raid.

Joey snuffling had me focusing down at my little baby snuggled up against my chest. I had him tucked under my shirt, so his warm little body was up against my bare skin. Grinning, I gently stroked a fingertip down his tiny cheek. He'd come out at a relatively healthy five pounds, four ounces. Big for a preemie, but with Scout as his father, it didn't come as a shock to me that he was bigger than he should be.

"Just like your papa, aren't you little man? Big and strong."

I couldn't wait to be able to take him home. To be able to spend my days with Ariel and Joey and my nights curled up in Scout's arms. That was my dream. To have all my family under the one roof, safe and sound. Running my finger over Joey's hand, I marveled at the softness of his skin. He was pure innocence right now. Completely dependent on me to give him what he needed. But I knew he'd grow up before I was ready. No doubt he'd grow up to be like his father, following him into the Charon MC.

As I watched my sweet boy sleep, I wasn't sure how I felt about that. Scout was the love of my life, but for so many years he'd denied me. One of the reasons he'd held back had been that he hadn't wanted me to be put at risk as the president's old lady. Turns out he was right to worry. The what ifs of what happened in the cafe tormented my mind. What if Ariel hadn't been able to get Cleo out? What if the men had panicked and just shot us all before running? What if Cindy hadn't come running with a bat like she was Harley Quinn?

Lifting my hand, I rubbed my stinging eyes. So many what ifs, so many worries for what would happen next time. Because no matter what Scout, or any of the club said, there would always be someone out there who wanted to come after the Charon MC.

"Love, don't cry."

Scout's strong arm went around my shoulders. I moved my hand away to look into his familiar face and I couldn't hold my tongue any more.

"What happens next time, Scout? What happens if Ariel's not there next time? And Cleo gets hurt? Is this our life—"

He cut me off by pressing his lips against mine, kissing me until the tension drained from my body.

"I promise you, I will do everything I can to make sure it never happens again. Whenever your cafe is open, or anyone is there, I'll have prospects protecting it, just like the other businesses in town where our people work. I'm not ever again assuming that Bridgewater is completely safe. I won't risk you like that. Never again."

I lifted the hand not cradling our son and stroked Scout's cheek before running my fingers through his beard. I didn't know how to respond to him. What could I say? That it was okay? That would be a lie. It wasn't okay that we needed around-the-clock security to feel safe. I didn't want to live like that. Nor did I know where all the prospects were going to come from. The Charons were going to have to do some serious recruiting to have enough manpower to accomplish everything he just declared.

"I don't want to have bodyguards follow me around forever, Scout. It'll make me feel trapped. And I know the other women will feel the same way. When there's a threat, sure, but not twenty-four/seven. And it's not fair to the prospects, which I don't believe the Charons have enough of, for all of that, anyhow. How about you teach me and the other old ladies how to shoot? I'll go to a few more of Mac's classes. Or maybe I should get Cindy to teach me how to swing a bat?"

Trying further to lighten the mood, I gave my man a smirk. Then grinned when he scoffed a chuckle and stood up to his full height as he shook his head.

"Cannot believe she came in swinging like that. Crazy-ass woman." He paused to sigh and run his hand through his hair. "Yeah, getting you and the other old ladies trained up sounds like a good plan. Mac actually suggested it a while back, but we never got around to making it happen. I'll bring it up at church next week, get things rolling. But you're not gonna be doing any of it until the doctor gives you the all clear. No way am I risking the recoil off a gun to damage you while you're healing up."

His words melted me. Always so focused on my wellbeing.

"Sure thing, babe. Now, get over here and kiss me."

"Yes, ma'am."

Since I couldn't easily stand, he leaned down and, bracing an arm on the wall behind my chair, he cupped my face with his other palm and took my mouth with his. Winding my free hand around the back of his neck, I threaded my fingers up into his hair as he deepened the kiss.

Joey squirmed and grunted and we broke apart. Chuckling, we both glanced down at our son, who hadn't appreciated the squish he'd been getting between us.

"Sorry, son."

Scout leaned down and pressed a kiss to the top of his head, making my eyes sting once more. *Wish I had my camera handy.*

Scout

I was on edge in a way I'd never been before. There was so much up in the air and none of it was within my ability to control. I hadn't heard from Arrow since he'd sent me a text to say they'd landed in New York earlier. He was due to call in each evening to keep me updated, so I wasn't expecting a call until later tonight. With any luck, he'd have some good news for me. Although, I didn't honestly expect them to have been able to sort much out in their first day up there, not when they went in with no fucking plan to start with.

But it wasn't just my club and the fact I wasn't able to go with them that had me on edge. Joey was still in the hospital. The doctor was talking like he needed to stay until his due date. Apparently that was protocol. I fucking hated it. Joey was doing well, I didn't understand why we couldn't just bring our boy home. I could tell Marie hated it as much as I did, and poor Ariel was getting shipped off to Bulldog's old lady, Rose, more days than not. Poor kid would start thinking we'd abandoned her again if this shit kept up.

Not to mention Marie's mental state. I knew full fucking well she was trying to hide it from me, but I could see it in her eyes. She was barely holding it together. Every now and then she'd let slip with something. Like last night when she was worried how I'd react to her c-section scar. Crazy woman. Like anything would change how much I loved her. If anything, every little thing she did made me love her more, never less. I mean, for real, she stayed calm while held at gunpoint. Held on for an extra week, despite Joey wanting to come out and see what all the commotion was about. That's what Marie had told me. Said he was just like me and wanted to see what was going on. She had a point. I'd always needed to know who was doing what around me and if anything was out of place, I did all I could to put it back where it was meant to be.

At least once this shit with Ice Riders and Sabella was dealt with, I could let the others take over running things for a week or two while I spent time with Marie, Ariel and Joey. Sadly, I didn't know how fucking long I'd have to wait for that, though. Everything was up in the air, from how long it would take to deal with the Ice Riders, to how long it would take to handle Sabella once that was finished.

My phone ringing had me stepping away from the bike I was working on, and when I saw it was Arrow calling through the secure app Keys set up for us, I headed to my office for some privacy. Him ringing this early could be good news, but I fucking doubted it.

The second I had the door shut, I answered the call.

"Talk to me."

"Not real sure what the fuck we've walked into up here. For a start, Parrish ain't the president anymore. Wolf has the top job now. He'll be calling you later."

That shocked me. "Was the change in leadership friendly?"

"Looks like. Although, Parrish still holds power and sway with the club. Actually, I feel sorry for Wolf. He's president, but he knows if Parrish wanted to, he'd put the call out and the club would ride for him in a heartbeat."

"Any news on the Riders?"

"In a way. The other thing we seemed to have walked in on up here is a war one of the local cartels—Sinaloa Cartel—has declared on the Knights. Shit escalated this morning and now the whole club's on lockdown. It's a fucking mess. But I think we can make it work. The Sinaloa Cartel is the one that the Riders are having trouble with. So, we're gonna go get the ledgers and go over them. See if we can find anything that we can use to tie up both loose ends. But, Scout, this cartel? The shit they're pulling? It's no joke. This is fucking war, brother. In all its bloody glory."

I winced and scrubbed my face with my palm. Fuck it all. I hadn't meant to send my men up into a fucking war zone.

"What you wanna do, Arrow? Is it worth staying? I don't want to lose men to another man's war."

"I wouldn't have volunteered to join this fight, brother. But now we're here, we're staying. These are good men and this fucking cartel is coming after their women. Old ladies, mothers, kids… they don't give a shit. They need to be stopped. And the Knights are gonna need all the help they can get."

I nodded, even though he couldn't see me. "Yeah, I hear you. Okay, get the ledgers and see what you find in them. But I don't want them to be left unattended. Put Bash on guard duty. They're never to leave his sight, understand?"

Last thing we needed was to have them go fucking missing, end up in the wrong hands that'll trace them back to Silk somehow.

"Understood. Not sure if there'll be much of any use in them. I mean, Mac didn't find anything obvious when he went through them earlier. Riggs, one of Wolf's men, is gonna go through them. Maybe a fresh set of eyes will see something we didn't."

"Yeah, maybe. Fucking things are nearly two decades old now. When you're done with them, burn 'em till they're dust. We got copies down here if we need anything that's in them again."

"Got it. Okay, I'd better get back to the fray and see what the fuck's going down now."

"Good deal. Stay safe, brother."

"Always. And, Scout?"

"Yeah?"

"Might wanna keep a bag packed. Something tells me this shit is gonna go down real soon and if you wanna be here for the final fight, you'll need to be here sooner, rather than later."

"If it's before Joey is released, I'll be there."

We said goodbye and hung up. Fuck, I hoped this shit would be over by the time my boy came home. Tucking the phone away, I went back to the bike and because my stupid ass was distracted, I slipped as I tried to undo the main nut on the rear wheel. My hand slammed against the belt guard and got sliced up at the base of my thumb.

"Motherfucker!"

Grabbing a cleanish looking rag, I used it to put some pressure on the wound as I headed to the bathroom to wash it up and get a better look at the damage.

"Boss, you all right?"

"Just cut my fucking hand up. Sure it'll be fine."

I knew Jazz would still follow me. He was a good kid, solid. And like Bash, way past due for his top rocker. After tossing the rag and giving it a thorough wash, the bitch was still bleeding. I'd hoped it wouldn't need stitches, but now I was pretty sure I wasn't getting that wish.

"Give me a look at it."

He sat the first aid kit on the bench and flipped it open as I held some paper towels against the slice across the base of my thumb.

Jazz winced when I lifted the blood-soaked paper to give him a look.

"Fuck, Scout. I think that's gonna need stitches."

Yeah, at this point I sadly agreed. Jazz was no medic, but I'd let him play the part for now. He was only trying to help. And the cut was on my right hand, so it would have been a struggle to get it done on my own, considering it was bleeding like a bitch.

"Do your best to close it up with some strips. I'll get Donna to look at it when I go to pick up Marie later."

I let my thoughts wander as I stood there waiting for him to finish up. Thoughts like the fact I probably shouldn't have even come in to the shop today. I definitely shouldn't have returned to work after that fucking phone call. What a mess. I'd sent men to a war, unintentionally, but still. They were there and I was here, being a fucking idiot and getting hurt in the process.

"Okay, you should be good to get to the hospital, at least. You got a cage, right? Not sure you'll be able to ride with it. And boss, I wouldn't leave it til later."

That was another thing—I hadn't been able to ride much lately. Someone always needed to be taken somewhere, so I was stuck in a fucking cage. And it was August. Fucking summer and I couldn't make the most of it. Although, we'd had a few scorchers when I'd certainly appreciated the air con. And I had no problem at all jumping in a cage to take my woman or my daughter wherever they needed to go.

"Yeah, I'll head in and get it looked at. Thanks, man."

Watching the red of my blood begin to bloom through the white bandage, I knew Jazz wasn't worth shit as a medic and I'd be heading straight in. Fuck it all. This was the last thing I needed. Grabbing some more paper towels, I put pressure on the wound as I made my way out to my car.

Confident the rest of my crew would clean up for me and finish off the job I was working on, along with keeping the shop running as they'd been doing for the past weeks, I palmed my keys and hopped in my cage.

It didn't take me long to get to the hospital. I swear at this point I could drive there with my eyes closed. Not that I'd try it. It also hadn't taken me long to locate

Donna, who was working at the main desk outside the ER.

"What the hell did you do to yourself this time?"

She stood in front of me with her hands on her hips and fire in her gaze that she had locked on to where I was back to applying pressure to my wound.

"Slipped working on a bike and cut up my hand. Might need a stitch or two, but I hope not."

She nodded. "Well, come with me and we'll see what the damage is this time." I followed her through the door into the ER. "This is rather novel, you coming into the hospital for treatment. Can't say I recall the last time that happened."

That had me chuckling. "I was coming in anyhow, so this time it was just easier for me to find you. You know how much we all appreciate how you come to us when we need it, right?"

I hoped she did. It was a Godsend having Donna on call like we did. I sat on the bed and held my hand out for her to cut away the shit Jazz had put on me.

"I know you do. And I hope you know how much I appreciate that you keep that bus so well stocked for me to work with."

Her frown deepened as she peeled all the shit Jazz had applied to my wound. I was scowling myself at it all. The boy must have used have the damn first aid kit. I should have paid more attention, rather than getting lost in my fucking head.

"Dare I ask who had a go at this?"

"Jazz. I wasn't watching him when he did it. Damn."

She shook her head as she tossed it all in the tray and set about cleaning the wound.

"Can you move your thumb okay?"

I flexed the digit in question and aside from the pain in the slice, it moved like normal.

"Good. Full movement. You could probably get away without stitches, but since I know how much you use your hands, I'm going to put a couple in to hold it together so it'll heal up better—and faster. You caught yourself a good one."

"Fucking main wheel nut wouldn't budge."

"And you're apparently too strong for your own good."

She cocked a brow at me, but I didn't respond. She probably had a point. If I'd thought about it for two seconds, rather than just putting more muscle—and anger— into it, I'd probably have avoided the injury all together.

With quick efficiency, Donna had me stitched and bandaged up. She stripped her gloves off and tossed them with everything else in the tray.

"Right. You've had stitches enough times to know the drill. Come back and see me to take them out, or just get one of the men to do it."

I gave her a nod and after standing up, leaned down to kiss her cheek.

"Thanks, darlin'. You're a gem."

"Yeah, yeah, save the charm for Marie. And gave that boy of yours a kiss for me. I haven't made it up there yet today."

Knowing Donna would keep my little visit off the books, I ducked out of the ER and made my way to the NICU to find my son and my woman, who was going to make a fuss over the fact I had a scratch.

Chapter 12

Marie

I hadn't been expecting Scout so soon. I definitely hadn't expected him to march in to the NICU with his hand all bandaged up. Since I'd been about to head to the bathroom, I'd just finished settling Joey back in his bassinet. After a final glance to make sure he was good, I turned my full attention to my man, who'd made his way to my side while I'd been looking the other way.

"What happened to your hand?"

"I slipped."

Crossing my arms over my chest, I raised an eyebrow at him. He knew that wasn't a good enough of an explanation for me.

"Gonna need more than that."

"That's the truth, babe. I was working on a bike and the nut wouldn't budge, so I put more muscle into it, and when the wrench slipped, my hand slammed into a sharp edge, slicing the base of my thumb open. It'll be fine. Donna just put a couple stitches in because it wouldn't quit bleeding."

Stitches? He wanted me to not worry when it was bad enough he'd needed to have it sewn up? Lost in thoughts of what really lay beneath the white gauze, I kept my gaze locked onto the bandages around his hand until he used his other hand to tilt up my chin. The moment I focused on his eyes, so blue and warm, he leaned down and took my lips with his. Kissing me slowly, gently, until the tension drained from my body and my hands pressed against his chest, taking a grip on the leather of his cut so he couldn't back away.

Until my bladder reminded me of what I was on my way to do before he interrupted me. Releasing my grip and smoothing down the leather, I stepped back.

"I need to go to the bathroom real quick."

He gave me a smirk and another quick kiss.

"Off you go. Us boys will just hang out here and wait for your return."

With a chuckle, I made my way out to the hallway and down to the bathroom.

When I returned to the NICU, bladder relieved, it was to Scout shirtless and a nurse helping get Joey settled on his bare chest. Before he saw me, I whipped out my phone and took a few snaps of them together. The look of complete love and adoration on Scout's face was something I'd never forget. I'd given him that. By having his baby, I was responsible for that look on his face right now. As I stepped closer, I took another couple photos on my phone and when he glanced up, his expression was priceless. His eyes sparkled with his joy, his lips stretched into a wide grin. That moment, right there, watching my man so at ease with our son, looking happier than I'd seen him in so long, made everything worth it.

Scout

I felt so much better after getting some cuddle time with Joey, but unfortunately I'd had to put him back in his crib and head out before I was ready to leave him. With a heavy heart, I took Marie's hand and left our son to go get our daughter. Once we had Ariel, we took her to get some flowers then headed over to the cemetery so she could visit with her momma. The guilt of not doing more to help Sarah sooner still ate at me, especially when we came here and I had to face her final resting place—glaring proof of how badly I'd fucked up.

Today a different emotion was stronger than the guilt, and when I saw that headstone it was determination that filled me. I would not allow Marie or any of the other old ladies see the same fate. I vowed to myself I would do whatever it took to end this current threat to my family, and any others that would come later. I would do everything in my power to make sure we had no one else to visit in this place.

"You're looking a little mean there, babe. What's on your mind?"

Marie's fingers ran over my chest as she stroked over my shirt until her hand was over my ribs, tucked into the warmth under my cut, as she moved to stand in front of me. Wrapping my arm around her, I brought her in closer, until she was pressed firmly against my front. Now she wasn't pregnant anymore, she fit in against me perfectly again, for which I was grateful. Nothing soothed me quite like having my woman in my arms, close enough my lungs were filled with nothing but her scent.

"I was just thinking about all I gotta do to make sure no one else I care about ends up here."

"You worried about the guys up in New York?"

I blew out a breath. Of course she'd know exactly what I was worried about, even though she didn't know about Arrow's call yet, she still knew.

"Yeah, that's part of it. Arrow called earlier. He thinks I'm going to need to head up there soon. Is that all right? I'll be as fast as I can. I don't want to leave you…"

I'd never been so fucking torn over what to do before. I didn't want to leave her and the kids, but I didn't want to leave taking out the Riders to anyone but me. As the president of the Charons, as Marie's man, as Joey and Ariel's father, I needed to be there when the final blow landed. It was just the way I was fucking wired.

Marie giving my beard a gentle tug had me moving my gaze from Ariel to her. Once she had my eyes on hers, she spoke.

"Scout, I know who I married. I know the caveman biker inside you wants to go and get vengeance for what happened. Just promise me if you do go, that you'll be careful. That you'll watch your back and not do anything stupid. I know you want to go help deliver vengeance, but I need you to come back to us in one piece more than I need you to go make those who hurt us pay. Because, Charlie, I need you more than I need justice or vengeance or anything else. Do you hear me?"

This woman wrecked me. How the fuck was I supposed to argue with that? Running my fingers over her cheek, I tucked her hair behind her ear.

"I hear you, love, loud and clear." I paused a moment to take in every inch of her beautiful face. A face I would never get tired of coming home to, waking up to. "I love you more than life, Marie. I'd never do a damn thing to risk not returning to you and the kids."

A tear slipped from her eye and after thumbing it away, I cradled her jaw and took her mouth, swiping my tongue in to tangle with hers when her lips parted on a sigh. Her taste filled me, fuelled me to keep kissing her. Arousal roared through my body, making my cock kick in my jeans. It'd been too long since I'd had her beneath me and I both missed and craved that connection with my woman. But it would be a long time yet til I got to slip inside her core. Her body needed time to heal first.

"Ew! You two are yucky!"

With a chuckle, we broke apart. Most of the time Ariel was still so damn quiet for a girl her age, and when she came out with stuff like she just did, it made my heart sing. It was such a normal thing for a five-year-old to say and gave me hope she was gonna cope just fine when she headed to school next month.

"C'mon, kiddo. Let's head home. What do you feel like for dinner?"

Scout

Waking with a jerk, I snapped out my hand for my phone, to hopefully answer the thing before it woke Marie. As I answered the call, I slipped out of the bed and, grabbing a pair of boxers from the floor, made my way down to the kitchen.

"Talk to me."

Considering it was one in the fucking morning, whoever it was calling me better have a damn good reason for it.

"Scout, Wolf over in New York. Sorry about the late hour but shit is heavy over here and, well, I don't gotta tell you how that goes."

Shoving the phone between my shoulder and ear, I stepped into my boxers before sitting down at the table, keeping my eye on the hallway in case either Marie or Ariel came in. This was not gonna be a conversation I wanted either of my girls overhearing.

"Got it. Tell me what's been going on? Arrow tells me you're the president now. That right?"

"Yeah, that's right but that's a story for another day. I'll tell ya this, though, the relationship between your club and the Knights will continue to thrive as if Jack were still the one holding the gavel. That being said, I appreciate you allowing us to have a look at those ledgers. I don't know how much your guys have told you but we got some shit going on here with the Sinaloa cartel. One of my guys caught a few mentions of them in those books of yours. Seems like they used to be the Ice Rider's drug supplier back in the day. Now, with these books being old as fuck we can't really ride on that. It's my understanding you didn't send your men here to break bread with the Riders, so I'm calling you to tell you we want in."

I was all for them helping us out on this. After all, the more men, the clearer the message. But I was quite sure Wolf wasn't making this offer out of the kindness of his heart. He wanted something out of this. So until I had some more facts, I wasn't agreeing to anything.

"Hold up. Why you got such a hard-on for this cartel?"

"You know how widespread the Sinaloa Cartel is. We had an altercation with their men in Queens. They declared war on Parrish. First with his wife and son, then today with his daughter. Broke into her and Blackie's house while she and Jack's son were asleep, tore it up, and painted the walls with blood, delivering a message."

A growl vibrated up my throat. "Are they okay? What'd the fuckers do?"

"They didn't touch them, thank fuck. But I've got my club on lockdown now and with Blackie in the can doing a bid and Jack on the brink of a fucking nervous breakdown, I gotta end this shit before bodies start dropping."

"Why the fuck are they coming after your women and kids and not touching any of you?" I scrubbed a hand over my face. "Seriously, this shit is so fucked up. I remember when a man's family was sacred."

"Time's change, brother. And not always for the better. I'm calling you because we ain't sitting on this shit. Since the Ice Riders have had dealings with them in the past, I want to go up to Boston with you and make those cocksuckers give up Javier's hit squad's current location. Once we get those pigs to squeal, we'll help you make the bastards pay for what they've done to you and yours. But I gotta tell you, Parrish ain't going to be contained for too much longer. If you want to play a role in the demise of the motherfuckers who wronged your woman, you need to be on the next flight here."

I shook my head. Their former president was losing his mind, literally, and they had one of the most prominent cartels going after their women and children. Not to mention one of their key players was in jail. Fuck. It made our issues down here seem tame.

"I gotta sort out someone to stay with my wife and daughter. She can't drive yet, after giving birth. But I'll get that done and be on the first flight up. I got a couple cuts I wanna toss at the feet of their fucking president before he goes to meet his maker."

"Good deal. Let me know when you're due to land and I'll send a cage to pick you up."

After hanging up I slid the phone onto the table and covered my face with my hands. I wanted to scream with how much I wished I could be in two fucking places at once right now.

"You need to go, don't you?"

I'd heard her pad across the room, so her voice and the warm palm on my shoulder didn't shock me. I dropped my hands away, scooting the chair back from the table as I pulled her down to sit in my lap.

"Yeah. Gonna need to fly up first thing in the morning. But I won't go until I know you've got someone here to look after you and Ariel."

She shrugged a shoulder like it was no big deal. "I'm sure Bulldog and Rose will be happy to come stay with me until you get back. How long do you think you'll be gone?"

"From the sounds of things, not long. Hopefully only a couple of days. If we're lucky, we'll get it all handled in one day and I'll be back tomorrow night."

I seriously doubted it, but a man could dream.

She ran her nose up my cheek as she gave my beard a small tug with her hand.

"Well, I guess we should get you back to bed for some sleep then, since you're no doubt going to be in for a full-on day tomorrow."

She slipped off my lap and my cock jerked to life as she took my hand and led me back to our bedroom. Never thought I'd consider a maternity bra and granny panties a turn on, but when that was all Marie was wearing? My dick was hard and throbbing in my boxers. How I wished I could take her back to bed, strip her off and fuck her hard. I had no clue what tomorrow would truly bring, how much danger I'd be in. Tonight might be the last time I had with her. I didn't want to think like that, but I couldn't help the thoughts from creeping in.

Kicking off my boxers as Marie laid down, I drank in the sight of her near-naked and spread out for me. She went to pull the covers over her but I stopped her, jerking them back down. She gave me a questioning look, flipping her gaze from my face to my cock.

"It's too soon, babe. No sex for another few weeks yet."

"Just 'cos I can't get my cock into you yet, don't mean I can't still play a little."

Her breath hitched and her cheeks grew pink as I lowered myself down next to her, running my hand down her body until I could slip under the edge of her panties. She was still bleeding a little, so I didn't even try to go any further than her clit. With just the tip of my finger, I gently teased the little nub. With a moan, she rolled on her side, and cupping my face in her palms, pulled me to her, initiating a kiss I soon took control of. I took her mouth like I wanted to take her pussy, thrusting my tongue in to dance with hers before retreating and doing it again.

One of her palms dropped from my face and she knocked my hand until I pulled out of her panties. But before I could voice my displeasure at losing my toy, my whole body jerked with pleasure as she wrapped those delicate fingers of hers around my cock and started stroking.

"Fuck, babe."

I rested my forehead against hers as she continued to tease me. I was on edge already, having gone way too long without a release. Then she let go and pushed my hip until I was laying on my back. Through half-closed eyes, I watched her as she crawled over me, her hair teasing the hell out of my chest as she purposely let it tickle my skin.

I wrapped my hand in the silk to move it out of the way as she got to where I wanted her and finally wrapped those lips I loved so much around my straining erection. I bit my lip to keep the groan from slipping out. The last thing I wanted was to wake Ariel right now.

Cupping my balls with her free hand, she worked me over like she'd gotten hold of my instruction manual and memorized every damn word of the thing. Every stroke, every touch and lick felt like heaven and before I was ready, my eyes rolled back and I jerked up, coming into her mouth.

I had the best old lady ever.

Once I'd got my senses back, I reached down and grabbed her shoulders to lift her up the bed so I could kiss her, loving how I got a little taste of myself because she'd swallowed me down.

"Fucking love you, Marie."

"Love you too, Charlie. Now, get some sleep. I don't want you getting hurt because you're too tired to function."

"Yes, ma'am."

I rolled over, killed the lamp then pulled her in against my body so I could spoon up behind her. As I drifted off, I sent up a prayer to whoever was listening that I would get to come back to her after we ended this shit up north.

Chapter 13

Scout

So far everything had run smoothly. Bulldog and Rose had come over first thing to stay with Marie and Ariel, and I'd gotten on the first flight out, no issue. I could only hope the trend continued.

Now I was standing outside Newark Airport, scanning the crowd at the pickup line for anyone wearing a Satan's Knights cut. When I finally saw one, I headed in the man's direction.

"You Scout?"

"Yeah, you got a name?"

"Nico, aka Satan's Knights' Bitch," he muttered as he tipped his chin toward the passenger seat. "Get in before Parrish cuts my dick off."

With a shake of my head and a chuckle, I opened the door, tossing my bag into the back before taking a seat. Then, before I had a chance to buckle my seatbelt, the crazy bastard had taken off from the curb and was weaving in and out of traffic, leaving me gripping the door handle.

"Fucking hell, are there always this many cars on the damn road?"

"Pretty much. Welcome to New York, cowboy."

"I ain't no cowboy. Wrong club, kid. We might do runs with the Satan's Cowboys MC but that's the end of it. We ain't them."

I was pretty sure he was just poking fun at me because I came from Texas, but no Charon would like being called a cowboy, so I figured it best to get that shit straight with Nico from the start.

"Hey, man, don't get your panties in a twist. I didn't even know that was a club."

I gave him a nod. "No harm done. We're good."

The rest of the ride passed in silence as I stared out the window at the insanity that was New York traffic. I was suddenly real fucking grateful I didn't have to attempt to navigate through this shit on my own.

When he pulled up in front of a bar and killed the engine, I wasn't sure what the fuck was going on.

"Thought we were going to your clubhouse?"

"Yeah, you're looking at it. Some fuckers blew up our old one a while back, now we meet here. One of the brothers owns it. We got rooms upstairs, cold beer on tap and the hottest fucking bartenders this side of the Verrazano. Pretty sweet deal."

He hopped out of the car before I could ask anything more about the whole blown-up-clubhouse thing so, I decided to let it drop for now. After grabbing my bag and slinging it over my shoulder, I followed his lead and trailed him up the path to the bar's main entrance.

"Honey, we're home!"

I smirked at Nico. Strange kid. Then made my way over to the bar where my brothers stood together.

"Hey, prez. Good to see you."

After giving each of the men a back slap I faced Arrow.

"Anything new happen since my early morning phone call from Wolf?"

Arrow nodded. "Plenty. We were waiting on you to come in before church was called."

He'd barely finished speaking when a shrill whistle filled the air.

"Get your asses to church. Charons, too."

Glancing over at the familiar voice, I winced when I saw Wolf. We really did look alike and I knew the boys were gonna give us hell for it. Once we all crowded into the small room behind the bar, Wolf banged a— I frowned and looked closer. Yep, his gavel was a fucking meat tenderizer. Silence reigned within moments.

Wolf stared me straight in the eye.

"Appreciate you getting here so fast. Those of you who aren't familiar, this here is Scout, the president of the Charon MC." After a couple seconds of mumbled greetings and head tilts, Wolf thankfully got into why we were here. I didn't want to waste time with this. Thoughts of Marie, Ariel and Joey had me on edge and even though I'd just arrived, I was already looking forward to going home. "All right, with that out of the way, let me catch you up to speed. Jack's old lady, Reina, got some of her memory back and she was able to confirm it was a black Cadillac that ran her into oncoming traffic."

"Motherfucking cunts."

Wolf raised an eyebrow at Jack's growled interruption before shaking his head and continuing on.

"As I was saying, Riggs is working on identifying the car. I also sent a couple of our guys to check out the addresses we found in the ledger. There's definitely activity going on over there..." I stood straighter as Wolf's gaze hardened while he stared me in the eye. "But we're going to need the Ice Riders to confirm before we send the intel down to the district attorney."

The fucking DA? Was he serious right now? What the fuck had we walked into here? A war with a cartel while they had the DA sniffing around? I kept my expression neutral, but inside I was reeling. And praying that when all the smoke cleared after this shit, we walked away without gaining any new enemies. It was for that reason I didn't ask for details on whatever they had going on with the DA. Ignorance truly was bliss in some situations.

I gave him a nod. "Two birds, one stone. So, what's the plan? We go shake down the Ice Riders for information before we wipe them out of existence? Because I'm more than happy to have me and my men help you out, but at the end of the day, I want the Ice Riders gone. Completely."

"Sounds fair. But we take the lead. Once we have what we need from them, you can come in and do whatever the fuck you want to whoever is left standing."

"I want Chains alive. Got a couple presents I want to deliver before he breathes his last."

Wolf shifted his gaze to Parrish. "You hear that? Man wants Chains alive, so keep your fucking head straight."

Parrish sneered his response as though I was asking him to stop breathing or something. "I'll see what I can do."

Not what I wanted to hear, but I was smart enough to know it was as good as I was going to get. And seriously, having the entirety of the Satan's Knights at our backs to deliver our vengeance was well worth the cost of maybe not being able to rub their president's nose in the fact we well and truly ended this war they stupidly fucking started with us.

"Jack, call Schwartz and see if he's gotten hold of Ritzer and the warden. If all is clear, we ride in ten."

I leaned back against the wall with my arms folded over my chest as Wolf continued on, barking out orders to various Knights to find cages and weapons for us to use and other things that needed to happen before we could head out.

I liked this plan. Felt comfortable following Wolf's lead to get what the Charon MC needed. What I wasn't so sure about, was getting involved with this fucking cartel business. Mob shit had always made me nervous. They had a nasty habit of coming back later to attempt to even the score, like Sabella was currently trying to do. But such was life. And this cartel had fucking gone after the Knights' women and children. Fuck that shit. Anyone who pulled that shit deserved to die and I, along with all the Charon MC, was more than happy to help the bastards to their royal reward.

Marie

Of course Bulldog and Rose had no problem coming over to stay with me while Scout was gone. Thankfully our house had a guest room already set up, so it was quick work to get them settled.

I was trying my best to not focus on what exactly Scout was doing each moment of the day, but I couldn't help it. He'd gone off to "end a war." He was putting himself in danger and I was worried sick he would get hurt. Especially since he was going in already injured. He'd taken off the bandages on his hand earlier this morning and it hadn't looked too bad. He'd left the stitches in and covered them with a couple of large Band Aids so it didn't look like he had more than a scratch. He assured me he would be careful.

"So what's on the schedule for today?"

Rose's voice pulled my attention from where I was aimlessly staring out the back windows of the house while I nursed my morning coffee.

"Ah, I guess I'll head into the hospital."

"When was the last time you baked?"

I turned to face Rose in surprise at the random question. "Um, not since before the raid. Why?"

I hadn't time. Or the desire, if I was being honest. She took my free hand and led me over to the couch. When she sat, I followed her lead, taking a sip of my coffee once I was seated.

"We can all see you're struggling, and I don't mean with what Scout's run off to do today. I'm not sure what's all ticking away in that head of yours, but what I do know, is you always used to bake your worries away. Maybe we should start that routine up again." She gave me a cheeky grin. "And I know the boys will certainly appreciate it down at your cafe if you start supplying the pies again. Don't get me wrong, the girls are doing their best, but no one makes pies like you do, darlin'."

Staying silent, I took another drink as I processed what Rose was saying. I'd been keeping all my doubts to myself, bottling them up, because I hadn't wanted to worry anyone. Apparently I hadn't been doing that great of a job of it, if everyone had noticed I was struggling.

"If you ever want to talk, I'm here for you. We all are. We're family, Marie, and we're all worried about you."

My eyes stung with tears as suddenly the pressure in my chest got too much to contain within me.

"I failed."

Rose jerked a little before leaning forward with a frown. "How on earth do you figure that?"

"I didn't carry Joey to full term. I couldn't birth him naturally. He's still in hospital *because I failed!*"

Her expression softened and I slipped my unfinished mug onto the end table so I could swipe away the tears that were now leaking from my eyes with both hands.

"Oh, sugar. I had no idea that's how you were feeling. Now you listen to me, Marie. You didn't fail at all. No one could have predicted those men were going to storm into your cafe like they did, and it sure as hell wasn't your fault. From what I've heard, you did incredibly well, staying calm, trying to talk them down. It wouldn't have taken much to push those two bastards the wrong way and to the point they simply shot everyone there and ran. You did good that day, Marie. The best you could, under the circumstances. And you delivered a healthy baby boy. Yeah, he's still in hospital, but from what you've told me, that's a precaution at this stage, not because there's anything majorly wrong with him. Many women elect to have a c-section these days. There is certainly no shame in having one. It was the best option to deliver Joey safely. You did all the right things, Marie. There's no failure in any of that."

I closed my eyes and pressed a palm over the scar. The one that Scout had told me he loved because I'd earned it birthing our son.

"I know all of that, I do. Scout keeps telling me. Donna too. But getting my head to accept it? That's the hard part."

I risked a glance up at Rose's face. As soon as she caught my gaze, she smiled gently.

"So, how about we see if some baking will help? Then we can deliver them down to the cafe. We'll sit down and stay for a coffee and try some of the pie. Spend some time being an adult before we go visit Joey later. You don't have to be there to feed him earlier than that, do you?"

I shook my head. "No, I've already expressed this morning and they have plenty of my breast milk at the hospital for him." I gave her a watery grin. "Turns out I'm a good cow."

Rose laughed, then rose to her feet, reaching for my hand to tug me up and into her arms where she gave me a quick, tight hug.

"You'll be just fine, Marie. I know it'll take a little time, but you'll get there. Now, let's get cooking. Where's Ariel at? I know she'll want to help."

She gave me a final squeeze before she left my side to go find Ariel, who'd been playing in her room the last time I'd checked on her. I appreciated the few minutes alone. It gave me a chance to quickly nip into the bathroom and splash some cold water on my face. I stayed in there a few extra moments, just taking some deep breaths and absorbing the fact I had the best friends in the world.

By the time I made it out to the kitchen where Rose was putting an apron on Ariel, I was smiling and ready to bake some pies.

"Alrighty, then. What flavor should we bake today, sweet angel?"

Chapter 14

Marie

Stepping foot back into my cafe was like coming home. I hadn't returned since the raid, not once. It was the longest I'd ever gone not coming in since I'd opened the doors all those years ago. Scout had assured me that Zara and Mercedes had it handled and I'd used that to be a coward, not wanting to return to the scene of the crime, so to speak. But it also meant that I'd missed out on everything I loved about my cafe. The atmosphere, the smells and sounds that had been so much of my world for the past twenty years.

"We're back! And with pies!"

Ariel made her loud declaration the moment she was through the door, making everyone in the place chuckle, myself included. Kids…

Zara and Mercedes both paused in what they were doing and came over to give me a hug. It wasn't that I hadn't seen either of them over the past weeks. They'd visited me in the hospital, and we all lived on the same street. But this was different. A sort of welcome home now that I'd finally put my big girl panties on and came in. Unexpectedly, emotion clogged my throat as I hugged them both in return. Thankfully, Ariel once more came to the rescue before it became obvious to everyone that I was having a moment.

"We made a pecan pie and a caramel pie. They smell sooo good. But Mommy wouldn't let me taste test them, so I can't tell you if they taste as good as they smell."

Zara kneeled down in front of Ariel and took the bag with the pies from her hands.

"Well, how about you go sit down with Mommy and we'll bring you over a little slice of each of them so you can work it out for us?"

Her face lit up and after sliding a quick glance at me, leaned in and loudly whispered to Zara. "Can I have a hot chocolate too? Please?"

I gave Zara a nod when she looked to me for approval before she stood and moved towards the counter where Mercedes had already returned. Taking Ariel's hand, I let her guide me to the table of her choosing with Rose following us.

"Baby Cleo isn't here today."

She sounded a little sad at that. And I frowned when I thought about it. Mac was up north, so who was looking after Cleo if she wasn't here? Rose spoke up with the answer. "I believe Silk and Eagle are on baby duty today." She paused and turned to face me. "Which reminds me, we really need to get working on our plan to open a child care center here in town."

I vaguely remembered her saying something about that in the hospital after we first found Ariel.

"We've certainly got the kids to populate one. And that's just the Charon kids. Open it up to the rest of the town, you've basically got a guaranteed success. Do you have a location in mind yet? And did you want to run it? It'll need a good, solid manager."

Rose sat back in her chair, clearly lost in thought while Zara set down drinks and pie for all of us.

"Can't tell you how good it is to see you here, Marie. This place just isn't the same without you."

I grinned up at her, pushing aside the guilt for staying away for so long. "It does feel good to be back. I didn't realize how much I was missing it, both baking and coming in, until Rose gave me a little push in that direction earlier. It'll be a little while before I can be on my feet long enough to be much good in here, but I'll definitely start baking again. And dropping in for more visits."

Baking those pies had done me a world of good. By the time they'd been in the oven and I was washing up the dishes as Rose and Ariel dried, I'd felt calmer and more settled than I had in weeks. I mean, I was still worried sick over Scout and what he was currently in the middle of, and I was still trying to accept how Joey's birth ended up happening, but I was in a much better place now than I was when I woke up this morning, that was for sure.

"I've got it!" I nearly dropped my mug of coffee at Rose's sudden outburst, but thankfully managed to recover before I made a mess and set it down to focus on my friend. "That vacant building a few doors down from the gym. It's been empty for years and if we set up there, we can set up a deal for people who want to work out at the gym to use us to look after their kids while they do. But I don't think I'd be the right person to run things. It's not like I'm qualified, or anything."

"You employ people qualified to take care of the kids. I dare say it would earn enough money to pay for a manager too, if needed. I just thought you'd like to be in charge of it since it was your idea."

She nodded as she thought over what I said.

"I guess at the very least I can oversee the set-up of things, until we can hire on staff. I'll get Bulldog to take it to the club. If they agree to fund it, it'll be much easier than trying to get a bank loan or something. And we can use the Charon manpower to get the place kitted out. I don't suppose you'd like to help me research what we'd need to put in there?"

My lips spread into a wide smile and excitement curled inside my stomach. "It sounds like the perfect project for us to work on while I'm recuperating."

"Excellent! We'll start this afternoon, after we go visit that gorgeous son of yours, of course."

Ideas were already swirling and as we both ate our pie and watched Ariel cut hers up as though she was conducting brain surgery on the thing.

"Mommy?"

"Yeah, angel?"

"I think next time we need to put in more nuts. The radio isn't quite right."

"It's ratio, spelt with a 't,' not a 'd,' and okay, we can try it with some extra nuts next time, sweetheart."

Rose was quietly chuckling at Ariel when I turned to face her again.

"Thank you so much for today. It was exactly what I needed. Truly, I can't thank you enough."

My stupid eyes were stinging again when Rose leaned forward and gave my arm a soft squeeze.

"It's what friends are for, Marie. No need to thank me. I know full well if the roles were reversed, you'd be doing the same exact thing for me."

That, I would. It really was a wonderful thing to have good people in your life.

Scout

Hanging back with the other Charons, we allowed the Knights to take the lead on storming the Ice Riders' clubhouse. If we hadn't known before, we definitely knew now that Jack Parrish was a fucking lunatic. Strapped with enough fucking weapons to fight a literal war, he marched to the front door, putting three bullets in the first unfortunate bastard that came through the portal, killing him before pulling a second gun free and entering the building with a number of the Knights at his heels. Gunfire instantly filled the air, but I didn't go to join the party just yet. As planned, I stayed outside with my men, waiting for the other Riders to arrive—assuming Parrish left any of them alive long enough to put the fucking call out for back-up. Our goal here was a clean sweep. The whole club taken down in one hit, so there was no one left to fucking come after us later.

Before long, the sounds of Harley engines filled the air and I glanced at my Charon brothers, and the Knights who had also stayed outside, to make sure everyone was loaded and ready to go as anticipation had my blood singing in my veins.

"First one is mine."

I got a few nods to my yell. Raising my gun, I took aim at the only entrance to the yard and waited. The moment a bike came through the open gates, I fired at the broad, exposed chest of the fucker riding it. A shiver ran through me, energizing me with the thrill of sending these bastards straight to hell, where they belonged. A grin tugged at my lips when the dead man and his ride went crashing into the line-up of bikes parked in front of the clubhouse, making one hell of a noise as every one of the Harleys fell over like dominos.

From there on out, it was chaos. Bikes kept coming through the gates, and bullets continued to fly, taking them out. We'd taken down eight men before we got a rider who was fast enough to pull a weapon and shoot back. Thankfully, he couldn't aim for shit and didn't hit anyone, and the fucker got taken down before he could get a second round off.

Once we couldn't hear any more bikes, we got busy checking that all the Ice Riders' we'd tagged were dead, finishing off any that were still breathing as we went. Then we got to the fun part of dragging their fucking bodies inside. The Ice Riders' compound was outside of town, but gunshots were loud, especially the amount of rounds we'd shot off. Since none of us knew the area or the people in it, we had no real fucking clue how long we had before the cops would show up. But no matter how time limited we were, we all knew we needed to gather all the evidence we could inside so when we blew the place up later, nothing would remain to come back to bite us in the ass. It also had the added benefit of Chains getting to see all his men lying dead at his feet while Parrish worked him over. Assuming Parrish hadn't lost his cool and killed the fucker already.

One of the Knights' prospects held the door open for us as we started dragging the fuckers inside. The first time I crossed the threshold, I froze for a moment at the blood bath. Fuck me. I'd seen some messed up shit in my time but in that moment I was fucking grateful I'd never ended up on the wrong side of Parrish. He had a pair of pliers and was literally ripping bits of Chains' ear off.

Turning away from the sight of Chains being tortured, I dropped my man to the side of the room, before heading back out to grab the next one. The trick to getting through shit like this, I found, was not thinking about it. Just get it done and move on. After I dropped the last body, I headed out to the loaner bike I'd ridden up here on and grabbed the cuts from the saddle bag before returning inside.

By the time I made it back into the main room of their clubhouse I had Tiny, Mac and Arrow with me. Bash had stayed behind at the Knights' clubhouse. Not only did I still have him on ledger guard duty, but he was young. He was better off not having to witness this level of carnage this early in his life. I'm sure the day would come when he'd take part, but for now, I felt better having him far away from it. I didn't stop until I was standing in front of Chains, the Ice Rider President. He'd been strapped down to a chair and Parrish had gone full Bulldog on him by the looks of things. One entire ear was missing and the whole side of his face was fucked up. Going by the bloody hammer, I'd say Parrish smashed his cheek and eye socket to hell with the thing.

Despite myself, I winced at the butchery. He had to be hurting like a motherfucker. Which was what I wanted, and what he deserved for all the shit he'd pulled on my club and family. I was grateful that despite all his injuries, the fucker was still conscious. I glanced briefly from him to his right, where Parrish stood, having just finished a phone call. Who the fuck was he ringing in the middle of all of this?

"You get the information you need yet, Bulldog?"

I keep my gaze on Chains as I waited for Parrish, aka Bulldog, to respond.

"Yeah. This cunt is all yours."

I sneered at the pathetic piece of shit before me. Mac and Tiny were still standing to either side of me as I tried to push past my fury at all the trouble this club had fucking caused me and mine. I needed to do this right. Show everyone around me I was still worthy of the president patch I wore.

I could tell by the bastard's body language he was just acting tough, with his jaw clenched tight and his shoulders up a little too high. Under the surface, he was on the verge of breaking down completely. Hell, fucker was tied to a chair and covered in explosives, his face fucked up and the bodies of his crew scattered around him. It was enough to have even the toughest of men feeling weak—and this fucker was not one of the toughest. No way.

I knew this operation had taken about all the time we could risk giving it already, but I wanted to take a few fucking seconds to soak this moment in—to let my brothers do the same.

This was sweet vengeance, Charon MC style.

"You didn't even know who the fuck I was, yet you came after my club. My pregnant old lady along with my brothers' women. Only a fucking idiot goes after a man and his club when he knows nothing about any of them. Let me clue you in. I'm the motherfucking president of the Charon MC, and you *do not* fuck with me or mine and live to speak about it." I held up the first of the cuts I'd brought in with me, making sure Chains got a good look at the name tag with his good eye. Then did the same with the second one before I laid both cuts carefully over his legs, making sure he could see both nametags, and the blood splatters that stained the leather around them. "You came after us for no fucking reason. We didn't do a fucking thing to bring down your wrath on us. But you came anyhow. And we will *never* stand idle when a threat shows up at our door."

His jaw clenched and his gaze narrowed on the leather in his lap, but he stayed silent. I figured he'd said all he was going to already, or maybe Parrish had broken his jaw and he couldn't speak. I didn't give a fuck. Everyone in this room knew he had nothing to say that could save his ass, or his club, at this point.

"Take a good fucking look around you, Chains. You did this. You took the fucking word of a mobster over three thousand miles away who you don't know from shit and came after us with guns blazing."

I moved forward, taking a handful of his hair, tilting his face up so he was forced to look me in the fucking eye rather than the cuts of his fallen brothers.

"You started this fucking war, but we're ending it. As of this moment, the Ice Riders MC is gone. History. Every single one of your brothers is dead or dying, and when we walk outta here, we'll hit the switch and your clubhouse will be nothing but fucking dust. Your precious club will be nothing but a cautionary tale on why you don't fuck with Charons or the Satan's Knights, because we will *always* fucking win."

With a growl, I released my hold on his hair and wiped my hand off on my jeans as I turned and walked out of there. I was done with all this shit. I had a woman and kids to get back to.

"Let's roll out. We've wasted enough time on these fucking fools."

As I pushed open the door I glanced back to see Parrish press his thumb on Chain's forehead and draw something. A cross maybe? Then he spat on the man before turning away. With a shake of my head I continued out to my loaner bike. So long as they blew this place straight to hell, I didn't give a fuck what the man did to the bastards within its walls prior.

With the air singing with the sound of all our Harleys roaring, Pipe hit the switch on the detonator before tossing the thing into the clubhouse's yard, it still sailing through the air when Wolf twirled his finger in the air and we all peeled away, riding down the street as the first explosion went off, shaking the ground beneath us for a moment.

It was done.

Vengeance had been served and this particular threat to me and mine was gone. I hoped Sabella heard about it. Heard about it and quaked in his fucking fancy-ass Italian loafers. Because the Charon MC was coming for his ass next.

Chapter 15

Marie

As grateful as I was for Scout's call to assure me it was all done and over, and that no Charons were injured, I wouldn't truly believe it until I laid my eyes on him. Taking the pie out of the oven and putting on the rack to cool, I glanced at the clock on the wall for the millionth time since he'd rung. He'd gotten the last seat on the six-thirty flight out of New York, so that had him landing in Houston at a little past twelve. It was currently about to click over one am. Bulldog had driven up to collect him, since I still couldn't drive, and hopefully they would get back any moment now.

This whole "can't do a damn thing for six weeks after surgery" thing was driving me crazy. I wished I could have gone to get my man personally. Been able to jump into his arms the moment he came through the gate, into the airport. But no, I was stuck here at home. With a sigh, I flipped the tap on to fill the sink. Seemed a waste to run the dishwasher for these few dishes, and honestly, I could use the distraction that washing them by hand gave me.

Since I'd already baked four pies tonight, I really didn't need to start another one. When Zara saw them all tomorrow, she might just call the psych ward on me.

Once done, I pulled the plug. The sound of the gurgling water was loud in the quiet room. So loud that I missed the front door opening. When I heard low male voices, I gasped and fled the kitchen, sprinting through the house toward the sound of Bulldog and Scout's murmured voices.

"What the fuck?"

He spun at the sound of my feet pounding against the hardwood floors. The second he saw me, a grin lit up his face and he held his arms out, catching me against his hard body when I crashed straight into him.

"I'll leave you to it and head up to Rose. Night."

I didn't give Bulldog any attention. I knew he'd understood. Instead I wrapped my arms around Scout's neck and buried my face into his beard, nuzzling until I found the soft skin there and kissed my way down to the edge of his shirt. With a growl, he gripped my ass and lifted me up. I wrapped my legs around his waist and he started moving, flipping off lights as he went through the house. He chuckled as he strode through the kitchen.

"Been baking, babe?"

"I was worried. It's what I do."

Making it to the bedroom, he loosened his grip and I lowered my feet to the floor.

"Well, it's what you used to do when you were stressin'. I'm glad you're back at it. Have to say, I was getting real worried about you, love. You haven't been your usual self since the attack. I hate that it was my fault—"

I put a finger over his mouth to stop him. "Don't you dare blame yourself for that. I know you don't tell me everything that goes on with the club, and honestly I don't want to know most of it. But I'm guessing you didn't actually do anything to bring those men to our door, right?"

He shook his head and pulled my hand away from his mouth. "It's a little complicated. But in short, the L.A. mob guy that came after Silk a couple years back told the Ice Riders we had some dirt on them and were planning to use it against them soon."

I shook my head as I tried to wrap my head around that one. "That still doesn't make any damn sense. Did they try to contact you at all prior to the attack? Are they going to try something else in the future?"

He shook his head no.

"What kind of person starts negotiations by holding innocents hostage?"

A new wave of rage flowed through me at how completely unnecessary the whole thing had been. I started pacing our room and going on a rant about how incredibly stupid those morons were. Not fully focused on what I was saying or where I was walking, I didn't realize Scout had stepped into my path until I walked into his chest.

"Babe. As cute as you are all riled up, there's no need. It's over. I don't normally tell you club business because you don't need to worry about any of it, but just so you can have peace of mind that they're not going to come back, I'll tell you a little. But don't go sharing this, even with the other old ladies.

"I agree with you. The Ice Riders should have just fucking called me, but they didn't. And now they don't exist anymore. That's what I was doing up north, babe. With the help of the Satan's Knights, we burned their club to the ground. We left no Ice Rider standing."

I tried to not wince at what he meant by "burned to the ground," and didn't want to know anything else about his trip up north. I rose up on my toes and pressed my lips to his, giving him a quick kiss and pulling away before he could deepen it and take control.

"If that's the kind of information I'm missing out on when you keep club business to yourself, then I'm more than happy for you to continue to keep me uninformed."

With a shake of his head and a small chuckle, he wrapped his arms around me. "Deal. Now, did you miss me?"

I rose an eyebrow and smirked up at him. "What? The sprinting through the house and jumping into your arms didn't make it clear?"

With a bark of laughter he leaned down and pressed a kiss to the corner of my mouth.

"Let me go get cleaned up, then we'll curl up and get some shut-eye. Because, Marie, I missed you like hell today, but I refuse to get in our bed all dirty from taking care of business."

I didn't say a word as he pressed another kiss to my lips before he released me and headed toward the bathroom. He paused near the hamper and stripped, gifting me with a view I'd never get tired of.

With a soft sigh, I watched his muscles flex and ripple as he got naked, then strode from the room. He left the door open so I shifted until I could keep him in my line of sight. I really was one lucky woman. He was strong, sexy as hell, as loyal as a man could get, and he loved me.

"You gonna just stand there watching, or you gonna come on in here and help me wash my back?"

I knew it wasn't his back that would be getting washed if I did join him, and I knew it wouldn't end how we both wanted it to either, because, dammit. I still had another five weeks until I could have sex. But I'd missed him like crazy and getting all wet and sliding up against his sexy body was too much temptation to resist.

I didn't take my time or draw out my stripping down. I just shed my clothes and strode into the bathroom, with a grin on my face and my heart about bursting for the man who held the door open for me while he got a glint in his eye I knew meant good things for us both.

※

Scout

Nothing beat sleeping wrapped around my woman. I was grateful I'd been able to make it back last night. Well, it was more like early this morning, but either way, I didn't have to spend a night sleeping away from Marie. And she'd stayed up waiting for me. I grinned as I remembered how she'd come barreling through the house before throwing herself at me. Now that was a homecoming I could get used to.

This morning had been equally enjoyable. I'd spent it at the hospital with my family, getting a cuddle from my baby boy, and watching as Ariel, completely in awe of her baby brother, got to hold him for a short while before Marie had to take him for a feeding.

But now it was afternoon and time to get back to club business. Since I'd only been able to get one ticket for the flight last night, the others had to stay up north until this morning. I'd sent Keys up in a cage to get them from the airport, letting Bulldog sleep in since he'd been the one to collect me in the wee hours of the morning. They were due to roll in any moment now. Later this afternoon we'd have a big family barbecue to celebrate, but before we got to the partying, I needed to grab Arrow for a quick chat, then we'd have church. After that, it would be relaxation time, at least for a short while. We still had business that needed to be taken care of before we could truly let our guard down for any length of time.

I was sitting at the bar nursing a beer, when the door swung open and they entered. I stood, making my way over to give each of them a back slap.

"Good to see you all got in safely. Sorry I couldn't get you home last night."

Arrow smirked and nudged Bash. "No problem, prez. Pretty sure it suited Bash, here, to have a few more hours in New York."

"Oh, yeah?" I raised my eyebrow and glanced toward the man who was blushing a deep red at Arrow's teasing. I remembered one of the Knights, Riggs, saying that Bash had been eyeing one of his bartenders. Guess from the color of his face right now, Bash got himself some lovin' before he left. Good on the kid. He deserved a reward for all the work he'd put in up there.

"Bash, all joking aside, you did good on this trip. We're having a barbecue later to celebrate. You're off the hook for any work. The other prospects can handle it all and you can sit back and enjoy the down time, yeah?"

"Thanks, prez. Can I head off till then? I need to check in on my mother."

I gave him a nod. "Of course. Family always comes first."

With a frown, I watched him run out of the clubhouse like his ass was on fire. Guilt ate at me that I hadn't spent more time with the kid. His mother had come to me nearly two years ago and asked me to watch out for him, as a favor to her deceased husband who'd served in the USMC with me. She'd had a brain tumor that had needed surgery and she wasn't sure she'd live through it. Naturally I'd agreed, and after meeting the man, I'd invited him to prospect with the club. He'd jumped at the chance and had proven his worth time and again. He was a quiet man though, and it hit me that I'd not taken the time to sit down with him to ask how he was, how his mother was doing. I knew she'd survived that initial surgery, but had she needed more since then?

I rubbed a palm over the back of my neck. Bash was well fucking overdue for his top rocker. Dammit. It felt like all we'd been doing for years now was putting out fucking fires. We hadn't put on a poker run, or even had that many family barbecues. That shit needed to change. We needed to get back to the core of what we were. Yeah, we protected our own and our town when trouble arrived, but we were also a fucking family. We needed to help each other out with the small stuff too, and celebrate the good.

With a sigh, I turned to Mac and Tiny, who both had moved to sit with their families, who'd been waiting with me for their return. Tiny had his woman in his lap, kissing the hell out of her. Mac had his daughter nestled in one arm while his other was wrapped around Zara, keeping her pressed up against his side as they sat on one of the couches.

"We got church in half hour so don't go running off too far."

I gave Arrow a nod and he followed me down to my office. Once the door was shut and we'd both taken a seat, I got straight to the point.

"How'd he do?"

"He did great. Handled everything he was thrown, like we knew he would. Kept his cool, even when Parrish was losing his. I think we should leave it until after we deal with Sabella to put it to a vote, but I'm confident he's a good choice for VP."

"You think he'll be able to handle shit in L.A.?"

Arrow shrugged a shoulder. "He's got a better chance than anyone else in the club at getting it done. He grew up there, used to be involved with the fuckers. Let him pick a team—at a guess that'll be Mac and Eagle, and give him the green light to get Sabella taken out and out of our lives for good."

I gave him a nod. That's what I'd been thinking of doing. Of course, we needed to run it by the club in church first, but I knew no one would object.

"We need to get this mob shit finished once and for all so we can get back to being us. Once Mac and his team are back home, we'll set up a poker run, have a big patch party for the prospects, and of course, for Mac."

"Assuming the vote passes."

Arrow was smirking as he spoke and I rolled my eyes at him.

"Like anyone will vote no on either Mac or any of the prospects. C'mon, let's get to church and get this shit done already."

It had only been about an hour since I'd seen them all, but I was already missing my wife and kids and wanted to be back with them. Strange how much my life had changed in the last year. I still loved my Charon family, still felt strongly about keeping them safe. Was still proud to wear the president patch. But Marie, Ariel and Joey were above that, they were now my first priority. And I wasn't complaining one bit. Nope, I fucking loved where my life had led me. If only all these crazy bastards after my club would leave me alone to enjoy it.

Epilogue

Five weeks later
Scout

The day had finally arrived. Marie had gone for her six-week check up with the doctor today and all was well. She'd healed up as she should have and we had a green fucking light.

We also had two kids at home, so the light could be fucking green all it liked, until we got them both in their beds, sleeping, I was fucked. Well, it was more a case of not being fucked, really. Not that I was truly complaining. As much as I wanted to be back inside Marie, I adored spending time with Ariel and Joey. Ariel loved being a big sister and was already super protective. Whenever we had visitors and they wanted to hold Joey, little Momma Bear Ariel was always there keeping a *very* close eye on the situation. Heaven help any kids at school who thought to pick on Joey when he was older. I could just see Marie and me getting hauled into the school because Ariel had knocked out some little bully who'd looked the wrong way at her baby brother.

Lord help us all if Cindy showed her how to swing a bat.

Speaking of the little munchkin, I'd just finished reading her a bedtime story.

"Right, sweet angel. Time for sleep."

"But, Papa, Mommy always reads me two stories."

She did? Since when? I raised my eyebrow at Ariel since this is the first time she'd mentioned this to me. Surely if Marie normally read her two stories, Ariel would have pulled me up on it when Marie had been in the hospital? But she didn't cave in to my stare, just looked up at me with her big, hazel eyes, pleading with me to read her another damn book. With a sigh, I relaxed, leaning back against her bed headboard as she snuggled in tight to my side and slipped another book into my hand. The kid came prepared for this whole two book thing, that's for sure. I'd ask Marie about it later. Not that it was a big deal or anything, I loved reading to Ariel. Even after all these months, she soaked up affection and information like a sponge.

Some nights she wanted a book that taught her about something. Like tonight. I'd just read her one all about a kid and her pet horse. Clearly the book was aimed to educate and Ariel had sat silently enthralled the entire time. I had my fingers crossed she didn't wake up in the morning and start begging us for a pony.

"Right, well, I guess another story it is, then. What are we reading, angel?"

I turned the book over and groaned at the cover. Dr. Seuss. Yeah, sometimes she just wanted some crazy silliness. Although, I had discovered there were actually some good life lessons in a lot of these Dr. Seuss books. Even Green Eggs and Ham, which is what it looked like I was reading tonight, had the underlying lesson of trying new things no matter how odd they might look. Not that we had that issue with Ariel—she'd eat anything we gave her. She was always so hungry for new experiences.

"C'mon, Papa. You do the *best* voices."

With a smile I opened the book to the first page. I loved doing stupid voices for her, making her giggle. I couldn't wait for Joey to be a little older, then I could have one of my kids on either side of me as I read to them while Marie watched on.

Who needed a fucking white picket fence to have it all? I had two happy, healthy kids and the best woman in the world as my wife. That was all a man needed. Sure, the nice house on a great street was good, as was the bike and car in the garage. But it wasn't what truly counted. It was the people in your life who completed you, that formed the legacy you would leave behind once you were gone. The men and women you called your family. And in that regard, I was extremely blessed. The Charon MC was one, huge family, and each one of them had my respect and came under my care. Which meant I felt every loss they suffered, too. My smile dropped for a moment as I thought about Bash once more. I hadn't known how bad his mother had gotten. Had been too caught up with all the fucking drama going on to see how much he'd been struggling. I'd failed in my promise to his mother, to him. I didn't think I'd ever fully forgive myself for it. But at least he'd found his place in the world now. Sucked it wasn't with a Charon MC cut on his back, but still, I knew Wolf would take good care of him up north.

Clearing my throat, I started the entertainment that was reading Green Eggs and Ham to my girl.

"I am Sam, Sam I am..."

Marie

After changing and feeding Joey, I was sitting in the rocker in his room, waiting for him to drop off to sleep when I heard Scout's deep rumble of a voice reading Green Eggs and Ham. A smile tugged at my lips as his voice pitched differently for each of the characters. That girl had her papa wrapped firmly around her little finger, that's for sure. Big, tough, Charon MC President, was in Ariel's overly girly room reading her Dr. Seuss complete with crazy voices...

I'd never loved him more.

"Your papa is the best, baby boy."

I lightly ran the tip of my finger over his round cheek. He had Scout's blue eyes and nose and I just knew he was going to grow up to be as handsome as his father. *Look out girls.*

Eventually he was soundly asleep to the point I could put him down. Carefully rising from the rocker, I walked to our bedroom and laid him in his bassinet where he snuffled a few moments before relaxing back into peaceful slumber. I stood watching him for who knows how long, just taking in each little rise and fall of his body as he breathed. He was just so beautiful—utter perfection. I could watch him forever.

"There's my woman."

Large hands slipped under my shirt and around until his arms were wrapped around my middle, pulling me back against him. I tilted my head when he nuzzled his face in against my shoulder then neck, his beard tickling my skin. Lifting my shirt to reveal his hands, I ran my palms over them, as we both stood there staring at our son. At least, we did until he started kissing his way up my neck, nibbling on my ear for a moment before whispering.

"I want you, Marie. So fucking bad. How about I move Joey to his room? We can bring him back in later, if you want."

I stiffened against him. "But he's only six weeks old, Scout. He's not—"

He cut me off by spinning me around in his arms and kissing me firmly on the lips before pulling back and staring me straight in the eye.

"Marie, love, I need you. You have no fucking idea how much I need to be inside you right now and I'm not gonna be quiet about it. And I'm not fucking you in front of our son. Ain't happening, babe. He's fast asleep, safely in his bassinet. He'll be fine. I, on the other hand, will not be fine if I don't get some lovin' from my woman in the next five minutes."

I wasn't entirely sure whether to laugh or not. He was being so adorably desperate. Not that I didn't understand where he was coming from. I'd missed making love with him so much over the past couple months.

"Fine, but please be careful. If he wakes now, he'll be up for hours."

I chewed my thumbnail as I watched Scout lift the bassinet from its base and walk out of our room. Jumping into action, I grabbed the base, and wheeling it along the floor, followed Scout to Joey's room. In silence, we got him all set up in there. I raised an eyebrow at Scout when he grabbed the baby monitor that we hadn't used yet, but apparently he'd taken the time to get all set up at some point today.

"I was optimistic about how tonight would go."

That did make me giggle. Then again when, with a low growl, he grabbed my hand and dragged me back to our bedroom, where he quietly shut our door. All levity left me when his heated gaze locked onto mine and stayed there.

"Strip, baby. 'Cos if you let me do it, I'm gonna tear the hell out of your clothes."

The desperate glint in his eyes, along with the rough way he started pulling his own clothes off, left me no doubt that he would, indeed, rip my clothes off if I let him. As mesmerizing as it was watching him strip down, I forced myself to focus on getting my own clothes off. Grateful we'd already gone over how much he didn't care about my new scar, I didn't hesitate to drop my panties. I carefully took my bra off and instantly cupped my heavy breasts in my palms. I'd only just fed Joey so I shouldn't leak all over the place, but I was still nervous I'd squirt all over Scout and ruin the mood.

"What'cha doing, babe?" He prowled up to me and slid his palms up my sides, coming in under my hands until he had my breasts cupped in his big palms and mine were wrapped around his wrists.

"They're sensitive. And bigger, heavier. I'm also kinda worried I might squirt milk at you."

He scoffed out a laugh before shaking his head at me with a grin. "Squirt all you like, love." He paused to wriggle his eyebrows at me and I couldn't help but laugh at the crazy man. "So long as I've got my hands and mouth on you, my cock in you, it won't bother me at all. And trust me, I've noticed how lush your body has become and I fucking *love* it."

He slipped his hands down again until he got to my waist and lifted. I wrapped my arms around his neck and my legs around his waist as he spun us until my back was against the wall. *Just like that first time back in that hotel in Houston.*

"Is this okay? I don't want to hurt you."

My eyes stung with tears. Even at his most desperate, when I knew what he really wanted was a long, hard fuck, he was holding back, making sure I was comfortable.

I cupped his face between my palms.

"I love you, Charlie Dalton. So much. My tummy's a little tender still, but other than that, and my boobs of course, I'm back to my normal self. Please, take me. You're not the only one that has been missing this. I want to feel you inside me so damn bad I'm about losing my mind!"

Before I could say more, he took my mouth with his as he lifted me up and lowered me down on his cock. A groan ripped up my throat at how good having this thick length within me felt. I clenched against him, caressing his dick with my walls until he was moaning and broke the kiss so he could stand back and start thrusting deeper.

I wrapped my fingers around his shoulders, digging my nails in as he sped up his tempo and my arousal spiraled higher. When he shifted his hips so he rubbed my clit with each thrust in, my body tightened on the verge of climax. Forgetting all about the kids, I opened my mouth to scream, but before I could make a sound Scout's lips were over mine, absorbing everything as I shuddered and came in his arms.

When the stars cleared from my vision I was lying on the bed, Scout over me with a big shit-eating grin on his face.

"Welcome back, babe."

With that, he thrust forward, filling me once more and making me realize he hadn't come when I had. With a moan I pushed my hips up, taking him as deep as I could. He moved to hold his weight on one arm and palmed my breast with the other, leaning down to wrap his lips around my nipple and tease the hard little nub. Running my fingers through his hair, I clutched him to me as my body continued to burn and spiral toward the edge of another climax.

"Charlie!"

"Let go, love. Let go and take me with you."

He took my mouth with his again and tweaked my nipple. The jolt of pleasure-pain enough to send me over the edge and once more, I screamed into his mouth. His thrusts sped up until, with a grunt he held still, his thick length pulsing inside me as he emptied himself. Moments later, he shifted off the bed and I rolled to my side, happily lost in bliss as I floated on my high. It wasn't until he returned and lifted my leg so he could clean me up that I realized I hadn't seen him put a condom on. Being the observant male he was, he picked up on my suddenly tensing up.

"Shit. Was I too rough, babe? Did I hurt you?"

I shook my head. "Not hurt, but did you put a condom on? Because I am so not ready to be pregnant again."

The relief reflected in his eyes confused me for a moment before he spoke.

"Thank fuck. You scared me for a minute there that I'd hurt you. I took you bare up against the wall, but I didn't come inside you then. I wrapped it up before I took you on the bed. We're all good, babe."

After tossing the cloth back into the bathroom, Scout slid onto the mattress and pulled me closer to him. With a contented sigh, I wriggled back against him as he tightened his arm around my torso, just under my breasts so he didn't hurt my still tender tummy, because that was the kind of man I'd married.

The best kind.

"Love you, Marie. Always and forever."

Yep, my man was totally the very best kind of male.

"I love you too, Charlie. Always have, always will."

He pressed a kiss in against my neck before he snuggled down to go to sleep. As I drifted off, my mind ran over all the things that had happened that led me to this moment and I decided that it was all worth it. All the loss and heartache and hard times were so very worth this paradise I found myself in. Wrapped in my man's arms while our two kids slept peacefully down the hall.

Life was good. It truly was.

The End

Other Charon MC Books:

Book 1:
Inking Eagle

The sins of her father will be her undoing... unless a hero rides to her rescue.

As the 15th anniversary of the 9/11 attacks nears, Silk struggles to avoid all reminders of the day she was orphaned. She's working hard in her tattoo shop, Silky Ink, and working even harder to keep her eyes and her hands off her bodyguard, Eagle. She'd love to forget her sorrows in his strong arms.

But Eagle is a prospect in the Charon MC, and her uncle is the VP. As a Daughter of the Club, she's off limits to the former Marine. But not for long. As soon as he patches in, he intends to claim Silk for his old lady. He'll wear her ink, and she'll wear his patch.

Too late, they learn that Silk's father had dark secrets, ones that have lived beyond his grave. When demons

from the past come for Silk, Eagle will need all the skills
he learned in the Marines to get his woman back safe,
and keep her that way.

Book 2:
Fighting Mac

She's no sleeping beauty, but then he's no prince - just a biker warrior to the rescue.

For the past three years Claire 'Zara' Flynn has been at the mercy of narcolepsy and cataplexy attacks. But after she witnesses a shooting by the ruthless Iron Hammers MC, her problems get a whole lot worse. She's now a marked woman, on the run for her life.

Former Marine Jacob 'Mac' Miller has a good life with the Charon MC. He works in the club gym and teaches self-defense classes - in the hopes of saving other women from the violent death his sister suffered. When the pretty new waitress at a local cafe catches his attention, he wants her in his bed. But there's a problem. She's clearly scared of all bikers. Wanting to help her, he talks her into coming to his class. Mac soon realizes he wants to keep her close in more ways than one. But can he, when his club's worst enemies come after her?

When Zara disappears, Mac and his brothers must go to war to get her back. Because this time, she wakes up in a terrible place... surrounded by other desperate women, and guarded by the Iron Hammers MC. Can her leather-clad prince ride to the rescue in time to save her from hell?

Book 3:
Chasing Taz

He lived his life one conquest at a time. She calculated her every move... until she met him.

Former Marine Donovan 'Taz' Lee might appear to be a carefree Aussie bloke living it up as a member of the Texan motorcycle club, Charon MC, but the truth is so much more complicated. With blood and tears haunting his past and threatening to destroy his future, Taz is completely unprepared for the woman of his dreams, when she comes in and knocks him on his ass. Literally.

Felicity "Flick" Vaughn joined the FBI to get answers behind her brother's dishonorable discharge and abandonment of his family. Knowing Taz was a part of her brother's final mission, she agrees to partner with him to go after a bigger club, The Satan's Cowboys MC.

However, nothing in life is ever simple and Flick is totally unprepared to have genuine feelings for the sexy

Aussie. When secrets are revealed and their worlds are busted wide open, will they be strong enough to still be standing when the dust settles?

Book 4:
Claiming Tiny

Some rules were meant to be broken.

After being raised in foster care, Ryan 'Tiny' Nelson has no plans to settle down. But that idea goes right out the window when Missy shows up at the clubhouse. One taste of the Charon MC's newest club whore and he's hooked.

Love is the last thing on Mercedes 'Missy' Soto's mind when she runs to the Charon MC for protection. But the first time Tiny wraps his arms around her, he captures her heart in the process.

When things start unravelling, Missy panics and runs. Will Tiny find her in time to give her a Christmas to remember, or will he lose her forever once her past catches up with her?

Book 5:
Saving Scout

Nothing worthwhile in life ever comes fast or easy.

Twenty five years after first meeting the Charon MC's president, Scout, Marie is still waiting for him to realize they're meant to be together. But instead, he comes to her asking she hire his ex. Frustrated with his continued rejection, she leaves town for the weekend to clear her head and maybe find a man who'll help her forget her infatuation.

When Scout first met Marie, she was way too young, and he hadn't been looking to settle down. Over the years, he'd never bothered to rethink his stance. When he learns Marie has fled town, he panics and realizes he needs to step up and claim what has always been his. Tracking her down, he approaches her at her hotel and he finally lets the sparks fly.

But before they can ride off into the sunset, trouble brews and Scout is taken by an enemy from their past that neither of them knew had been waiting for them. Can they overcome this latest hurdle to finally find their happily ever after? Or are they doomed to always be apart?

Book 6:
Tripping Nitro

Sometimes the one that got away comes
Back... bringing trouble with her.

It's really her. Former Navy SEAL and member of Charon MC, Nitro can't believe his eyes when he finds his high school girlfriend in a bar nineteen years after she disappeared, taking his heart with her.

Alone and running from a stalker since she was 16 years old, Cindy has avoided all contact with the opposite sex in order to keep her mysterious stalker appeased. Now, with Nitro by her side, he vows to keep both her body and heart protected, but can she risk believing him?

With the help of his Charon MC brothers, Nitro keeps Cindy guarded while he attempts to woo her back into his arms. But just when he manages to break through her walls, she vanishes again. Will Nitro be able to put together all the pieces of the puzzle in time to save his first and only true love?

CPSIA information can be obtained
at www.ICGtesting.com
Printed in the USA
BVHW040232260321
603416BV00006B/725